Jane Eyre: An Autobiography

Currer Bell, Smith, Elder and Co.

BIBLIOLIFE

JANE EYRE.

An Autobiography.

EDITED BY

CURRER BELL.

IN THREE VOLUMES.
VOL. III.

LONDON:
SMITH, ELDER AND CO., CORNHILL.
——
1847.

JANE EYRE.

CHAPTER I.

SOME time in the afternoon I raised my head, and looking round and seeing the westering sun gilding the sign of its decline on the wall, I asked, " What am I to do?"

But the answer my mind gave—" Leave Thornfield at once"—was so prompt, so dread, that I stopped my ears: I said, I could not bear such words now. " That I am not Edward Rochester's bride, is the least part of my woe," I alleged: " that I have wakened out of most glorious dreams, and found them all void and vain, is a horror I could bear and master; but that I must leave him decidedly, instantly, entirely, is intolerable. I cannot do it."

But, then, a force within me averred that I could do it; and foretold that I should do it. I wrestled with my own resolution: I wanted to be weak that I might avoid the awful passage of further suffering I saw laid out for me; and conscience, turned tyrant, held passion by the throat, told her, tauntingly, she had yet but dipped her dainty foot in the slough, and swore that with that arm of iron, he would thrust her down to unsounded depths of agony.

"Let me be torn away, then!" I cried, "Let another help me!"

"No; you shall tear yourself away; none shall help you: you shall, yourself, pluck out your right eye; yourself cut off your right hand: your heart shall be the victim; and you, the priest, to transfix it."

I rose up suddenly, terror-struck at the solitude which so ruthless a judge haunted,—at the silence which so awful a voice filled. My head swam as I stood erect: I perceived that I was sickening from excitement and inanition; neither meat nor drink had passed my lips that day, for I had taken no breakfast. And, with a strange pang, I now reflected that, long as I had been shut up here, no message had been sent to ask how I was, or to invite me to come down: not even little Adèle had tapped at the door; not even Mrs. Fairfax had sought me. "Friends always forget those whom fortune forsakes," I murmured, as I undrew the bolt and passed out. I stumbled over an obstacle: my head was still dizzy, my sight was dim and my limbs were feeble. I could not soon recover myself; I fell, but not on to the ground: an out-stretched arm caught me; I looked up—I was supported by Mr. Rochester, who sat in a chair across my chamber threshold.

"You come out at last," he said. "Well, I have been waiting for you long, and listening; yet not one movement have I heard, nor one sob: five minutes' more of that death-like hush, and I should have forced the lock like a burglar. So, you shun me?—you shut yourself up and grieve alone? I would rather you had come and up-braided me with vehemence. You are passionate: I expected a scene of some kind. I was prepared for the hot rain of tears; only I wanted them to be shed on my breast: now a senseless floor has received them, or your drenched handkerchief. But I err: you have not wept at all! I see a white cheek and a faded eye, but no trace of tears. I suppose, then, your heart has been weeping blood?

"Well, Jane; not a word of reproach? Nothing bitter—nothing poignant? Nothing to cut a feeling or sting a passion? You sit quietly where I have placed you, and regard me with a weary, passive look.

"Jane, I never meant to wound you thus. If

B 2

the man who had but one little ewe lamb that was
dear to him as a daughter, that ate of his bread
and drank of his cup, and lay in his bosom, had
by some mistake slaughtered it at the shambles,
he would not have rued his bloody blunder more
than I now rue mine. Will you ever forgive
me?"

Reader!—I forgave him at the moment, and on
the spot. There was such deep remorse in his
eye, such true pity in his tone, such manly energy
in his manner; and, besides, there was such unchanged love in his whole look and mein—I forgave him all: yet not in words, not outwardly;
only at my heart's core.

"You know I am a scoundrel, Jane?" ere long
he inquired wistfully—wondering, I suppose, at my
continued silence and tameness; the result rather
of weakness than of will.

"Yes, sir."

"Then tell me so roundly and sharply—don't
spare me."

"I cannot: I am tired and sick. I want some
water." He heaved a sort of shuddering sigh, and
taking me in his arms, carried me down stairs.
At first I did not know to what room he had borne
me; all was cloudy to my glazed sight: presently
I felt the reviving warmth of a fire; for, summer
as it was, I had become icy cold in my chamber.

He put wine to my lips; I tasted it and revived; then I ate something he offered me, and was soon myself. I was in the library—sitting in his chair —he was quite near. "If I could go out of life now, without too sharp a pang, it would be well for me," I thought; "then I should not have to make the effort of cracking my heart-strings in rending them from among Mr. Rochester's. I must leave him, it appears. I do not want to leave him—I cannot leave him."

"How are you now, Jane?"

"Much better, sir: I shall be well soon."

"Taste the wine again, Jane."

I obeyed him; then he put the glass on the table, stood before me, and looked at me attentively. Suddenly he turned away, with an inarticulate exclamation, full of passionate emotion of some kind: he walked fast through the room and came back; he stooped towards me as if to kiss me: but I remembered caresses were now forbidden. I turned my face away, and put his aside.

"What!—How is this?" he exclaimed hastily. "Oh, I know! you won't kiss the husband of Bertha Mason? You consider my arms filled, and my embraces appropriated?"

"At any rate, there is neither room nor claim for me, sir."

"Why, Jane? I will spare you the trouble of

much talking: I will answer for you—because I have a wife already, you would reply.—I guess rightly?"

"Yes."

"If you think so, you must have a strange opinion of me: you must regard me as a plotting profligate —a base and low rake who has been simulating disinterested love in order to draw you into a snare deliberately laid, and strip you of honour, and rob you of self-respect. What do you say to that? I see you can say nothing: in the first place, you are faint, still, and have enough to do to draw your breath; in the second place, you cannot yet accustom yourself to accuse and revile me; and, besides, the flood-gates of tears are opened, and they would rush out if you spoke much; and you have no desire to expostulate, to upbraid, to make a scene: you are thinking how *to act—talking*, you consider, is of no use. I know you—I am on my guard."

" Sir, I do not wish to act against you," I said; and my unsteady voice warned me to curtail my sentence.

" Not in *your* sense of the word—but in *mine*, you are scheming to destroy me. You have as good as said that I am a married man—as a married man you will shun me, keep out of my way: just now you have refused to kiss me. You intend to make yourself a complete stranger to me; to live under this roof only as Adèle's governess: if ever I say a friendly word to you; if ever a friendly feeling inclines you again to me, you will say,—'That man had nearly made me his mistress: I must be ice and rock to him;' and ice and rock you will accordingly become."

I cleared and steadied my voice to reply : " All is changed about me, sir; I must change too— there is no doubt of that; and, to avoid fluctuations of feeling, and continual combats with recollections and associations, there is only one way— Adèle must have a new governess, sir."

" Oh, Adèle will go to school—I have settled that already: nor do I mean to torment you with the hideous associations and recollections of Thornfield Hall—this accursed place—this tent of Achan—this insolent vault, offering the ghastliness of living death to the light of the open sky— this narrow stone hell, with its one real fiend, worse than a legion of such as we imagine.—Jane, you shall not stay here, nor will I. I was wrong ever to bring you to Thornfield Hall, knowing as I did how it was haunted. I charged them to conceal from you, before I ever saw you, all knowledge of the curse of the place; merely because I feared Adèle never would have a governess to stay if she knew with what inmate she was housed, and

my plans would not permit me to remove the
maniac elsewhere—though I possess an old house,
Ferndean Manor, even more retired and hidden
than this, where I could have lodged her safely
enough, had not a scruple about the unhealthiness
of the situation, in the heart of a wood, made my
conscience recoil from the arrangement. Probably
those damp walls would soon have eased me of
her charge : but to each villain his own vice ; and
mine is not a tendency to indirect assassination,
even of what I most hate.

" Concealing the mad-woman's neighbourhood
from you, however, was something like covering a
child with a cloak, and laying it down near a upas-
tree : that demon's vicinage is poisoned, and always
was.   But I'll shut up Thornfield Hall : I'll nail
up the front door, and board the lower windows ;
I'll give Mrs. Poole two hundred a year to live
here with *my wife,* as you term that fearful hag :
Grace will do much for money, and she shall have
her son, the keeper at Grimsby Retreat, to bear
her company and be at hand to give her aid in the
paroxysms, when *my wife* is prompted by her
familiar to burn people in their beds at night, to
stab them, to bite their flesh from their bones, and
so on."—

" Sir," I interrupted him, "you are inexorable
for that unfortunate lady : you speak of her with

hate—with vindictive antipathy. It is cruel—she cannot help being mad."

"Jane, my little darling, (so I will call you, for so you are), you don't know what you are talking about; you misjudge me again : it is not because she is mad I hate her. If you were mad, do you think I should hate you?"

"I do indeed, sir."

"Then you are mistaken, and you know nothing about me, and nothing about the sort of love of which I am capable. Every atom of your flesh is as dear to me as my own : in pain and sickness it would still be dear. Your mind is my treasure, and if it were broken, it would be my treasure still: if you raved, my arms should confine you, and not a strait waistcoat—your grasp, even in fury, would have a charm for me : if you flew at me as wildly as that woman did this morning, I should receive you in an embrace, at least as fond as it would be restrictive. I should not shrink from you with disgust as I did from her : in your quiet moments you should have no watcher and no nurse but me; and I could hang over you with untiring tenderness, though you gave me no smile in return; and never weary of gazing into your eyes, though they had no longer a ray of recognition for me.— But, why do I follow that train of ideas? I was talking of removing you from Thornfield. All, you know, is prepared for prompt departure : to-morrow you shall go. I only ask you to endure one more night under this roof, Jane; and then, farewell to its miseries and terrors for ever! I have a place to repair to which will be a secure sanctuary from hateful reminiscences, from un-welcome intrusion—even from falsehood and slander."

"And take Adèle with you, sir," I interrupted; "she will be a companion for you."

"What do you mean, Jane? I told you I would send Adèle to school: and what do I want with a child for a companion? and not my own child,—a French dancer's bastard. Why do you importune me about her? I say, why do you assign Adèle to me for a companion?"

"You spoke of a retirement, sir; and retirement and solitude are dull : too dull for you."

"Solitude! Solitude!" he reiterated, with irri-tation. "I see I must come to an explanation. I don't know what sphynx-like expression is form-ing in your countenance. *You* are to share my solitude. Do you understand?"

I shook my head: it required a degree of cou-rage, excited as he was becoming, even to risk that mute sign of dissent. He had been walking fast about the room, and he stopped, as if suddenly rooted to one spot. He looked at me long and hard: I turned my eyes from him, fixed them on the fire, and tried to assume and maintain, a quiet, collected aspect.

"Now for the hitch in Jane's character," he said at last, speaking more calmly than from his look I had expected him to speak. "The reel of silk has run smoothly enough so far; but I always knew there would come a knot and a puzzle: here it is. Now for vexation, and exasperation, and endless trouble! By God! I long to exert a fraction of Samson's strength, and break the entanglement like tow!"

He recommenced his walk: but soon again stopped, and this time just before me.

"Jane! will you hear reason?" (he stooped and approached his lips to my ear) "because, if you won't, I'll try violence." His voice was hoarse; his look that of a man who is just about to burst an insufferable bond and plunge headlong into wild licence. I saw that in another moment, and with one impetus of frenzy more, I should be able to do nothing with him. The present—the passing second of time—was all I had in which to control and restrain him: a movement of repulsion, flight, fear, would have sealed my doom—and his. But I was not afraid: not in the least. I felt an inward power; a sense of influence, which supported me. The crisis was perilous; but not without its charm : such as the Indian, perhaps, feels when he slips over the rapid in his canoe. I took hold of his clenched hand; loosened the contorted fingers; and said to him, soothingly,—

"Sit down; I'll talk to you as long as you like, and hear all you have to say, whether reasonable or unreasonable."

He sat down : but he did not get leave to speak directly. I had been struggling with tears for some time : I had taken great pains to repress them, because I knew he would not like to see me weep. Now, however, I considered it well to let them flow as freely and as long as they liked. If the flood annoyed him, so much the better. So I gave way, and cried heartily.

Soon I heard him earnestly entreating me to be composed. I said I could not while he was in such a passion.

"But I am not angry, Jane : I only love you too well; and you had steeled your little pale face with such a resolute, frozen look, I could not endure it. Hush, now, and wipe your eyes."

His softened voice announced that he was subdued; so I, in my turn, became calm. Now he made an effort to rest his head on my shoulder : but I would not permit it. Then he would draw me to him : no.

"Jane! Jane!" he said—in such an accent of bitter sadness, it thrilled along every nerve I had; "you don't love me, then? It was only my station, and the rank of my wife, that you valued? Now that you think me disqualified to become your husband, you recoil from my touch as if I were some toad or ape."

These words cut me: yet what could I do or say? I ought probably to have done or said nothing: but I was so tortured by a sense of remorse at thus hurting his feelings, I could not control the wish to drop balm where I had wounded.

"I *do* love you," I said, "more than ever: but I must not show or indulge the feeling; and this is the last time I must express it."

"The last time, Jane! What! do you think you can live with me, and see me daily, and yet, if you still love me, be always cold and distant?"

"No, sir; that I am certain I could not; and therefore I see there is but one way: but you will be furious if I mention it."

"Oh, mention it! If I storm, you have the art of weeping."

"Mr. Rochester, I must leave you."

"For how long, Jane? For a few minutes, while you smooth your hair—which is somewhat dishevelled; and bathe your face—which looks feverish ?"

"I must leave Adèle and Thornfield. I must part with you for my whole life : I must begin a new existence amongst strange faces and strange scenes."

"Of course : I told you you should. I pass over the madness about parting from me. You mean you must become a part of me. As to the new existence, it is all right; you shall yet be my wife : I am not married. You shall be Mrs. Rochester—both virtually and nominally. I shall keep only to you so long as you and I live. You shall go to a place I have in the south of France : a white-walled villa on the shores of the Mediterranean. There you shall live a happy, and guarded, and most innocent life. Never fear that I wish to lure you into error—to make you my mistress. Why do you shake your head? Jane, you must be reasonable; or in truth I shall again become frantic."

His voice and hand quivered; his large nostrils dilated; his eye blazed : still, I dared to speak :—

"Sir, your wife is living : that is a fact acknowledged this morning by yourself. If I lived with you as you desire, I should then be your mistress : to say otherwise is sophistical — is false."

"Jane, I am not a gentle-tempered man—you forget that: I am not long-enduring; I am not cool and dispassionate. Out of pity to me and yourself, put your finger on my pulse, feel how it throbs, and—beware!"

He bared his wrist, and offered it to me: the blood was forsaking his cheek and lips, they were growing livid; I was distressed on all hands. To agitate him thus deeply, by a resistance he so abhorred, was cruel: to yield was out of the question. I did what human beings do instinctively when they are driven to utter extremity—looked for aid to one higher than man: the words "God help me!" burst involuntarily from my lips.

"I am a fool!" cried Mr. Rochester, suddenly. "I keep telling her I am not married, and do not explain to her why. I forget she knows nothing of the character of that woman, or of the circumstances attending my infernal union with her. Oh, I am certain Jane will agree with me in opinion, when she knows all that I know! Just put your hand in mine, Janet—that I may have the evidence of touch as well as sight, to prove you are near me—and I will in a few words show you the real state of the case. Can you listen to me?"

"Yes, sir: for hours if you will."

"I ask only minutes. Jane, did you ever hear,

or know, that I was not the eldest son of my house: that I had once a brother older than I?"

"I remember Mrs. Fairfax told me so once."

"And did you ever hear that my father was an avaricious, grasping man?"

"I have understood something to that effect."

"Well, Jane, being so, it was his resolution to keep the property together; he could not bear the idea of dividing his estate and leaving me a fair portion: all, he resolved, should go to my brother, Russell. Yet as little could he endure that a son of his should be a poor man. I must be provided for by a wealthy marriage. He sought me a partner betimes. Mr. Mason, a West India planter and merchant, was his old acquaintance. He was certain his possessions were real and vast: he made inquiries. Mr. Mason, he found, had a son and daughter; and he learned from him that he could and would give the latter a fortune of thirty-thousand pounds: that sufficed. When I left college, I was sent out to Jamaica, to espouse a bride already courted for me. My father said nothing about her money; but he told me Miss Mason was the boast of Spanish Town for her beauty: and this was no lie. I found her a fine woman, in the style of Blanche Ingram; tall, dark, and majestic. Her family wished to secure me, because I was of a good race; and so did she.

They showed her to me in parties, splendidly dressed. I seldom saw her alone, and had very little private conversation with her. She flattered me, and lavishly displayed for my pleasure her charms and accomplishments. All the men in her circle seemed to admire her and envy me. I was dazzled, stimulated: my senses were excited; and being ignorant, raw, and inexperienced, I thought I loved her. There is no folly so besotted that the idiotic rivalries of society, the prurience, the rashness, the blindness of youth, will not hurry a man to its commission. Her relatives encouraged me; competitors piqued me; she allured me: a marriage was achieved almost before I knew where I was. Oh—I have no respect for myself when I think of that act!—an agony of inward contempt masters me. I never loved, I never esteemed, I did not even know her. I was not sure of the existence of one virtue in her nature: I had marked neither modesty, nor benevolence, nor candour, nor refinement in her mind or manners— and, I married her:—gross, grovelling, mole-eyed blockhead that I was! With less sin I might have —but let me remember to whom I am speaking.

"My bride's mother I had never seen: I understood she was dead. The honey-moon over, I learned my mistake: she was only mad; and shut up in a lunatic asylum. There was a younger

brother, too; a complete dumb idiot. The elder
one, whom you have seen (and whom I cannot
hate, whilst I abhor all his kindred, because he has
some grains of affection in his feeble mind; shown
in the continued interest he takes in his wretched
sister, and also in a dog-like attachment he once
bore me), will probably be in the same state one
day. My father, and my brother Russell, knew
all this; but they thought only of the thirty thousand pounds, and joined in the plot against me.

" These were vile discoveries; but, except for
the treachery of concealment, I should have made
them no subject of reproach to my wife: even
when I found her nature wholly alien to mine;
her tastes obnoxious to me; her cast of mind common, low, narrow, and singularly incapable of
being led to anything higher, expanded to anything larger—when I found that I could not pass
a single evening, nor even a single hour of the
day with her in comfort; that kindly conversation
could not be sustained between us, because, whatever topic I started, immediately received from
her a turn at once coarse and trite, perverse and
imbecile—when I perceived that I should never
have a quiet or settled household, because no servant would bear the continued outbreaks of her
violent and unreasonable temper, or the vexations
of her absurd, contradictory, exacting orders—

even then I restrained myself: I eschewed up-
braiding, I curtailed remonstrance; I tried to
devour my repentance and disgust in secret; I
repressed the deep antipathy I felt.

"Jane, I will not trouble you with abominable
details: some strong words shall express what I
have to say. I lived with that woman up-stairs
four years, and before that time she had tried me
indeed: her character ripened and developed with
frightful rapidity; her vices sprung up fast and
rank: they were so strong, only cruelty could
check them; and I would not use·cruelty. What a
pigmy intellect she had—and what giant propensities! How fearful were the curses those propensities entailed on me! Bertha Mason,—the true
daughter of an infamous mother,—dragged me
through all the hideous and degrading agonies
which must attend a man bound to a wife at once
intemperate and unchaste.

" My brother in the interval was dead; and at
the end of the four years my father died too. I
was rich enough now—yet poor to hideous indigence: a nature the most gross, impure, depraved
I ever saw, was associated with mine, and called
by the law and by society a part of me. And I
could not rid myself of it by any legal proceedings;
for the doctors now discovered that *my wife* was
mad—her excesses had prematurely developed

the germs of insanity :—Jane, you don't like my
narrative; you look almost sick—shall I defer the
rest to another day ?"

" No, sir ; finish it now : I pity you—I do
earnestly pity you."

" Pity, Jane, from some people, is a noxious and
insulting sort of tribute, which one is justified in
hurling back in the teeth of those who offer it : but
that is the sort of pity native to callous, selfish hearts:
it is a hybrid, egotistical pain at hearing of woes,
crossed with ignorant contempt for those who have
endured them. But that is not your pity, Jane : it
is not the feeling of which your whole face is full
at this moment—with which your eyes are now
almost overflowing—with which your heart is
heaving—with which your hand is trembling in
mine. Your pity, my darling, is the suffering
mother of love : its anguish is the very natal pang
of the divine passion. I accept it, Jane : let the
daughter have free advent—my arms wait to
receive her."

" Now, sir, proceed : what did you do when
you found she was mad?"

" Jane—I approached the verge of despair : a
remnant of self-respect was all that intervened
between me and the gulf. In the eyes of the
world I was doubtless covered with grimy dishonour : but I resolved to be clean in my own

sight—and to the last I repudiated the contamina-
tion of her crimes, and wrenched myself from
connexion with her mental defects. Still, society
associated my name and person with hers; I yet
saw her and heard her daily: something of her
breath (faugh!) mixed with the air I breathed;
and, besides, I remembered I had once been her
husband—that recollection was then, and is now,
inexpressibly odious to me: moreover, I knew
that while she lived I could never be the husband
of another and better wife; and, though five years
my senior, (her family and my father had lied to
me even in the particular of her age), she was
likely to live as long as I, being as robust in frame
as she was infirm in mind. Thus, at the age of
twenty-six, I was hopeless.

" One night I had been awakened by her yells
—(since the medical men had pronounced her
mad, she had of course been shut up)—it was a
fiery West-Indian night; one of the description
that frequently precede the hurricanes of those
climates: being unable to sleep in bed, I got up
and opened the window. The air was like sul-
phur-steams—I could find no refreshment anywhere. Mosquitoes came buzzing in and hummed
sullenly round the room; the sea, which I could
hear from thence, rumbled dull like an earthquake
—black clouds were casting up over it; the moon

was setting in the waves, broad and red, like a hot cannon-ball—she threw her last bloody glance over a world quivering with the ferment of tempest. I was physically influenced by the atmosphere and scene, and my ears were filled with the curses the maniac still shrieked out; wherein she momentarily mingled my name with such a tone of demon-hate, with such language!—no professed harlot ever had a fouler vocabulary than she: though two rooms off, I heard every word—the thin partitions of the West-India house opposing but slight obstruction to her wolfish cries.

"'This life,' said I at last, 'is hell! this is the air —those are the sounds of the bottomless pit! I have a right to deliver myself from it if I can. The sufferings of this mortal state will leave me with the heavy flesh that now cumbers my soul. Of the fanatic's burning eternity I have no fear: there is not a future state worse than this present one—let me break away, and go home to God!'

"I said this while I knelt down at, and unlocked a trunk which contained a brace of loaded pistols: I meant to shoot myself. I only entertained the intention for a moment; for, not being insane, the crisis of exquisite and unalloyed despair which had originated the wish and design of self-destruction, was past in a second.

"A wind fresh from Europe blew over the ocean

and rushed through the open casement: the storm broke, streamed, thundered, blazed, and the air grew pure. I then framed and fixed a resolution. While I walked under the dripping orange-trees of my wet garden, and amongst its drenched pomegranates and pine-apples, and while the refulgent dawn of the tropics kindled round me—I reasoned thus, Jane:—and now listen; for it was true Wisdom that consoled me in that hour, and showed me the right path to follow.

" The sweet wind from Europe was still whispering in the refreshed leaves, and the Atlantic was thundering in glorious liberty: my heart, dried up and scorched for a long time, swelled to the tone, and filled with living blood—my being longed for renewal—my soul thirsted for a pure draught. I saw Hope revive—and felt Regeneration possible. From a flowery arch at the bottom of my garden I gazed over the sea—bluer than the sky: the old world was beyond; clear prospects opened, thus :—

" ' Go,' said Hope, ' and live again in Europe: there it is not known what a sullied name you bear, nor what a filthy burden is bound to you. You may take the maniac with you to England; confine her with due attendance and precautions at Thornfield: then travel yourself to what clime you will, and form what new tie you like. That

woman, who has so abused your long-suffering—
so sullied your name; so outraged your honour;
so blighted your youth—is not your wife; nor are
you her husband. See that she is cared for as her
condition demands, and you have done all that
God and humanity require of you. Let her
identity, her connection with yourself, be buried
in oblivion: you are bound to impart them to no
living being. Place her in safety and comfort:
shelter her degradation with secrecy, and leave
her.'

"I acted precisely on this suggestion. My
father and brother had not made my marriage
known to their acquaintance; because, in the
very first letter I wrote to apprise them of the
union—having already begun to experience ex-
treme disgust of its consequences; and from the
family character and constitution, seeing a hideous
future opening to me—I added an urgent charge
to keep it secret: and very soon, the infamous
conduct of the wife my father had selected for
me, was such as to make him blush to own her as
his daughter-in-law. Far from desiring to publish
the connection, he became as anxious to conceal
it as myself.

"To England, then, I conveyed her: a fearful
voyage I had with such a monster in the vessel.
Glad was I when I at last got her to Thornfield,

and saw her safely lodged in that third story
room, of whose secret inner cabinet she has now
for ten years made a wild beast's den—a goblin's
cell. I had some trouble in finding an attendant
for her; as it was necessary to select one on
whose fidelity dependence could be placed; for
her ravings would inevitably betray my secret:
besides, she had lucid intervals of days—sometimes
weeks—which she filled up with abuse of me. At
last I hired Grace Poole, from the Grimsby Retreat. She and the surgeon, Carter (who dressed
Mason's wounds that night he was stabbed and
worried), are the only two I have ever admitted to
my confidence. Mrs. Fairfax may indeed have
suspected something; but she could have gained
no precise knowledge as to facts. Grace has, on
the whole, proved a good keeper: though, owing
partly to a fault of her own, of which it appears
nothing can cure her, and which is incident to
her harassing profession, her vigilance has been
more than once lulled and baffled. The lunatic
is both cunning and malignant; she has never
failed to take advantage of her guardian's temporary lapses: once to secrete the knife, with
which she stabbed her brother, and twice to possess herself of the key of her cell, and issue
therefrom in the night-time. On the first of
these occasions, she perpetrated the attempt to

burn me in my bed : on the second she paid that ghastly visit to you. I thank Providence, who watched over you, that she then spent her fury on your wedding apparel; which perhaps brought back vague reminiscences of her own bridal days : but on what might have happened, I cannot endure to reflect. When I think of the thing which flew at my throat this morning, hanging its black and scarlet visage over the nest of my dove, my blood curdles——."

"And what, sir," I asked, while he paused, "did you do when you had settled her here? Where did you go?"

"What did I do, Jane? I transformed myself into a Will-o'-the-wisp. Where did I go? I pursued wanderings as wild as those of the March-spirit. I sought the Continent, and went devious through all its lands. My fixed desire was to seek and find a good and intelligent woman, whom I could love : a contrast to the fury I left at Thornfield——."

"But you could not marry, sir."

"I had determined and was convinced that I could and ought. It was not my original intention to deceive, as I have deceived, you. I meant to tell my tale plainly, and make my proposals openly : and it appeared to me so absolutely rational that I should be considered free to love and be loved, I never doubted some woman might be found willing and able to understand my case and accept me, in spite of the curse with which I was burdened."

" Well, sir ?"

" When you are inquisitive, Jane, you always make me smile. You open your eyes like an eager bird, and make every now and then a restless movement; as if answers in speech did not flow fast enough for you, and you wanted to read the tablet of one's heart. But before I go on, tell me what you mean by your ' Well, sir?' It is a small phrase very frequent with you; and which many a time has drawn me on and on through interminable talk : I don't very well know why."

" I mean,—What next ? How did you proceed? What came of such an event ?"

" Precisely: and what do you wish to know now ?"

" Whether you found any one you liked: whether you asked her to marry you; and what she said."

" I can tell you whether I found any one I liked, and whether I asked her to marry me : but what she said is yet to be recorded in the book of Fate. For ten long years I roved about, living first in one capital, then another: sometimes in St. Petersburg; oftener in Paris; occasionally in

Rome, Naples, and Florence. Provided with plenty of money, and the passport of an old name, I could choose my own society: no circles were closed against me. I sought my ideal of a woman amongst English ladies, French countesses, Italian signoras, and German Gräfinnen. I could not find her. Sometimes, for a fleeting moment, I thought I caught a glance, heard a tone, beheld a form, which announced the realization of my dream: but I was presently undeceived. You are not to suppose that I desired perfection, either of mind or person. I longed only for what suited me—for the antipodes of the Creole: and I longed vainly. Amongst them all I found not one, whom, had I been ever so free, I—warned as I was of the risks, the horrors, the loathings of incongruous unions—would have asked to marry me. Disappointment made me reckless. I tried dissipation—never debauchery: that I hated, and hate. That was my Indian Messalina's attribute: rooted disgust at it and her restrained me much, even in pleasure. Any enjoyment that bordered on riot seemed to approach me to her and her vices, and I eschewed it.

" Yet I could not live alone: so I tried the companionship of mistresses. The first I chose was Céline Varens—another of those steps which make a man spurn himself when he recalls them.

You already know what she was, and how my liaison with her terminated. She had two successors: an Italian, Giacinta, and a German, Clara; both considered singularly handsome. What was their beauty to me in a few weeks? Giacinta was unprincipled and violent: I tired of her in three months. Clara was honest and quiet; but heavy, mindless, unimpressible: not one whit to my taste. I was glad to give her a sufficient sum to set her up in a good line of business, and so get decently rid of her. But, Jane, I see by your face you are not forming a very favourable opinion of me just now. You think me an unfeeling, loose-principled rake: don't you?"

"I don't like you so well as I have done sometimes, indeed, sir. Did it not seem to you in the least wrong to live in that way: first with one mistress and then another? You talk of it as a mere matter of course."

"It was with me; and I did not like it. It was a grovelling fashion of existence: I should never wish to return to it. Hiring a mistress is the next worst thing to buying a slave: both are often by nature, and always by position, inferior; and to live familiarly with inferiors is degrading. I now hate the recollection of the time I passed with Céline, Giacinta, and Clara."

I felt the truth of these words; and I drew

from them the certain inference, that if I were so
far to forget myself and all the teaching that had
ever been instilled into me, as—under any pretext—with any justification—through any temptation—to become the successor of these poor
girls, he would one day regard me with the same
feeling which now in his mind desecrated their
memory. I did not give utterance to this conviction: it was enough to feel it. I impressed it
on my heart, that it might remain there to serve
me as aid in the time of trial.

"Now, Jane, why don't you say 'Well, sir?'
I have not done. You are looking grave. You
disapprove of me still, I see. But let me come to
the point. Last January, rid of all mistresses—
in a harsh, bitter frame of mind, the result of a
useless, roving, lonely life—corroded with disappointment, sourly disposed against all men, and
especially against all *woman*kind (for I began to
regard the notion of an intellectual, faithful, loving
woman as a mere dream), recalled by business, I
came back to England.

"On a frosty winter afternoon, I rode in sight
of Thornfield Hall. Abhorred spot! I expected
no peace—no pleasure there. On a stile in Hay-
lane I saw a quiet little figure sitting by itself. I
passed it as negligently as I did the pollard willow
opposite to it: I had no presentiment of what it

would be to me; no inward warning that the arbitress of my life—my genius for good or evil—waited there in humble guise. I did not know it, even when, on the occasion of Mesrour's accident, it came up and gravely offered me help. Childish and slender creature! It seemed as if a linnet had hopped to my foot and proposed to bear me on its tiny wing. I was surly; but the thing would not go: it stood by me with strange perseverance, and looked and spoke with a sort of authority. I must be aided, and by that hand: and aided I was.

" When once I had pressed the frail shoulder, something new—a fresh sap and sense—stole into my frame. It was well I had learnt that this elf must return to me—that it belonged to my house down below — or I could not have felt it pass away from under my hand, and seen it vanish behind the dim hedge, without singular regret. I heard you come home that night, Jane: though probably you were not aware that I thought of you, or watched for you. The next day I observed you—myself unseen—for half an hour, while you played with Adèle in the gallery. It was a snowy day, I recollect, and you could not go out of doors. I was in my room; the door was ajar: I could both listen and watch. Adèle claimed your outward attention for awhile; yet

I fancied your thoughts were elsewhere : but you were very patient with her, my little Jane; you talked to her and amused her a long time. When at last she left you, you lapsed at once into deep reverie : you betook yourself slowly to pace the gallery. Now and then, in passing a casement, you glanced out at the thick-falling snow; you listened to the sobbing wind, and again you paced gently on, and dreamed. I think those day-visions were not dark : there was a pleasureable illumination in your eye occasionally, a soft excitement in your aspect, which told of no bitter, bilious, hypochondriac brooding : your look re-vealed rather the sweet musings of youth, when its spirit follows on willing wings the flight of Hope, up and on to an ideal heaven. The voice of Mrs. Fairfax speaking to a servant in the hall wakened you : and how curiously you smiled to and at yourself, Janet! There was much sense in your smile : it was very shrewd, and seemed to make light of your own abstraction. It seemed to say—' My fine visions are all very well, but I must not forget they are absolutely unreal. I have a rosy sky, and a green flowery Eden in my brain; but without, I am perfectly aware, lies at my feet a rough tract to travel, and around me gather black tempests to encounter.' You ran down-stairs and demanded of Mrs. Fairfax some occupation: the weekly house-accounts to make up, or something of that sort, I think it was. I was vexed with you for getting out of my sight.

" Impatiently I waited for evening, when I might summon you to my presence. An unusual— to me—a perfectly new character I suspected was yours: I desired to search it deeper, and know it better. You entered the room with a look and air at once shy and independent; you were quaintly dressed—much as you are now. I made you talk: ere long I found you full of strange contrasts. Your garb and manner were restricted by rule; your air was often diffident, and altogether that of one refined by nature, but absolutely unused to society, and a good deal afraid of making herself disadvantageously conspicuous by some solecism or blunder; yet, when addressed, you lifted a keen, a daring, and a glowing eye to your inter- locutor's face: there was penetration and power in each glance you gave; when plied by close ques- tions, you found ready and round answers. Very soon, you seemed to get used to me—I believe you felt the existence of sympathy between you and your grim and cross master, Jane; for it was astonishing to see how quickly a certain pleasant ease tranquillized your manner: snarl as I would, you showed no surprise, fear, annoyance, or dis- pleasure at my moroseness; you watched me, and now and then smiled at me with a simple yet sagacious grace I cannot describe. I was at once content and stimulated with what I saw: I liked what I had seen, and wished to see more. Yet, for a long time, I treated you distantly, and sought your company rarely. I was an intellectual epicure, and wished to prolong the gratification of making this novel and piquant acquaintance: besides, I was for a while troubled with a haunting fear that if I handled the flower freely its bloom would fade—the sweet charm of freshness would leave it. I did not then know that it was no transitory blossom ; but rather the radiant resemblance of one, cut in an indestructible gem. Moreover, I wished to see whether you would seek me if I shunned you—but you did not; you kept in the school-room as still as your own desk and easel : if by chance I met you, you passed me as soon, and with as little token of recognition, as was consistent with respect. Your habitual expression in those days, Jane, was a thoughtful look: not despondent, for you were not sickly; but not buoyant, for you had little hope, and no actual pleasure. I wondered what you thought of me—or if you ever thought of me: to find this out, I resumed my notice of you. There was something glad in your glance, and genial in your manner, when you conversed: I saw you had a social heart; it was the silent school-room—it was the tedium of your life that made you mournful. I permitted myself the delight of being kind to you; kindness stirred emotion soon: your face became soft in expression, your tones gentle; I liked my name pronounced by your lips in a grateful, happy accent. I used to enjoy a chance meeting with you, Jane, at this time: there was a curious hesitation in your manner; you glanced at me with a slight trouble—a hovering doubt: you did not know what my caprice might be—whether I was going to play the master and be stern, or the friend, and be benignant. I was now too fond of you often to simulate the first whim; and, when I stretched my hand out cordially, such bloom and light and bliss rose to your young, wistful features, I had much ado often to avoid straining you then and there to my heart."

"Don't talk any more of those days, sir," I interrupted, furtively dashing away some tears from my eyes: his language was torture to me; for I knew what I must do—and do soon—and all these reminiscences, and these revelations of his feelings, only made my work more difficult.

"No, Jane," he returned: "what necessity is there to dwell on the Past, when the Present is so much surer—the Future so much brighter?"

I shuddered to hear the infatuated assertion.

"You see now how the case stands—do you not?" he continued. "After a youth and manhood, passed half in unutterable misery and half in dreary solitude, I have for the first time found what I can truly love—I have found *you*. You

are my sympathy—my better self—my good angel
—I am bound to you with a strong attachment.
I think you good, gifted, lovely: a fervent, a
solemn passion is conceived in my heart; it
leans to you, draws you to my centre and spring
of life, wraps my existence about you—and, kindling in pure, powerful flame, fuses you and me
in one.

"It was because I felt and knew this, that I
resolved to marry you. To tell me that I had
already a wife is empty mockery: you know now
that I had but a hideous demon. I was wrong to
attempt to deceive you; but I feared a stubbornness
that exists in your character. I feared early
instilled prejudice: I wanted to have you safe
before hazarding confidences. This was cowardly:
I should have appealed to your nobleness and
magnanimity at first, as I do now—opened to you
plainly my life of agony—described to you my
hunger and thirst after a higher and worthier existence—shown to you, not my *resolution* (that word
is weak) but my resistless *bent* to love faithfully and
well, where I am faithfully and well loved in
return. Then I should have asked you to accept my
pledge of fidelity, and to give me yours: Jane—
give it me now."

A pause.

"Why are you silent, Jane?"

I was experiencing an ordeal: a hand of fiery
iron grasped my vitals. Terrible moment: full

of struggle, blackness, burning! Not a human being that ever lived could wish to be loved better than I was loved; and him who thus loved me I absolutely worshipped: and I must renounce love and idol. One drear word comprised my intolerable duty—" Depart !"

" Jane, you understand what I want of you? Just this promise—' I will be yours, Mr. Rochester.'"

" Mr. Rochester, I will *not* be yours."

Another long silence.

" Jane !" recommenced he, with a gentleness that broke me down with grief, and turned me stone-cold with ominous terror—for this still voice was the pant of a lion rising—" Jane, do you mean to go one way in the world, and to let me go another ?"

" I do."

" Jane," (bending towards and embracing me) " do you mean it now ?"

" I do."

" And now ?" softly kissing my forehead and cheek.

" I do—" extricating myself from restraint rapidly and completely.

" Oh, Jane, this is bitter ! This—this is wicked. It would not be wicked to love me."

" It would to obey you."

A wild look raised his brows—crossed his features: he rose; but he forbore yet. I laid my hand on the back of a chair for support: I shook, I feared—but I resolved.

"One instant, Jane. Give one glance to my horrible life when you are gone. All happiness will be torn away with you. What then is left? For a wife I have but the maniac up-stairs: as well might you refer me to some corpse in yonder churchyard. What shall I do, Jane? Where turn for a companion, and for some hope?"

"Do as I do: trust in God and yourself. Believe in heaven. Hope to meet again there."

"Then you will not yield?"

"No."

"Then you condemn me to live wretched, and to die accursed?" His voice rose.

"I advise you to live sinless; and I wish you to die tranquil."

"Then you snatch love and innocence from me? You fling me back on lust for a passion—vice for an occupation?"

"Mr. Rochester, I no more assign this fate to you than I grasp at it for myself. We were born to strive and endure—you as well as I: do so. You will forget me before I forget you."

"You make me a liar by such language: you sully my honour. I declared I could not change: you tell me to my face I shall change soon. And what a distortion in your judgment, what a perversity in your ideas, is proved by your conduct! Is it better to drive a fellow-creature to despair than to transgress a mere human law—no man being injured by the breach? for you have neither relatives nor acquaintances whom you need fear to offend by living with me."

This was true: and while he spoke my very Conscience and Reason turned traitors against me, and charged me with crime in resisting him. They spoke almost as loud as Feeling: and that clamoured wildly. " Oh, comply !" it said. " Think of his misery ; think of his danger—look at his state when left alone : remember his head-long nature ; consider the recklessness following on despair—soothe him ; save him ; love him : tell him you. love him and will be his. Who in the world cares for *you?* or who will be injured by what you do?"

Still indomitable was the reply—" *I* care for myself. The more solitary, the more friendless, the more unsustained I am, the more I will respect myself. I will keep the law given by God ; sanc-tioned by man. I will hold to the principles received by me when I was sane, and not mad—as I am now. Laws and principles are not for the times when there is no temptation : they are for such moments as this, when body and soul rise in mutiny against their rigour : stringent are they ; inviolate they shall be. If at my individual convenience I might break them, what would be their worth ? They have a worth—so I have always believed ; and if I cannot believe it now,

it is because I am insane—quite insane: with my
veins running fire, and my heart beating faster
than I can count its throbs. Preconceived
opinions, foregone determinations, are all I have
at this hour to stand by: there I plant my
foot."

I did. Mr. Rochester, reading my countenance, saw I had done so. His fury was wrought
to the highest: he must yield to it for a moment,
whatever followed; he crossed the floor and
seized my arm, and grasped my waist. He
seemed to devour me with his flaming glance:
physically, I felt, at the moment, powerless as
stubble exposed to the draught and glow of a
furnace—mentally, I still possessed my soul, and
with it the certainty of ultimate safety. The
soul, fortunately, has an interpreter—often an
unconscious, but still a truthful interpreter—in the
eye. My eye rose to his; and while I looked in
his fierce face, I gave an involuntary sigh: his
gripe was painful, and my over-tasked strength
almost exhausted.

"Never," said he, as he ground his teeth,
"never was anything at once so frail and so
indomitable. A mere reed she feels in my hand!
(and he shook me with the force of his hold.) I
could bend her with my finger and thumb: and
what good would it do if I bent, if I uptore, if
I crushed her? Consider that eye: consider the
resolute, wild, free thing looking out of it, defy-

ing me, with more than courage—with a stern triumph. Whatever I do with its cage, I cannot get at it—the savage, beautiful creature! If I tear, if I rend the slight prison, my outrage will only let the captive loose. Conqueror I might be of the house; but the inmate would escape to heaven before I could call myself possessor of its clay dwelling-place. And it is you, spirit—with will and energy, and virtue and purity—that I want: not alone your brittle frame. Of yourself, you could come with soft flight and nestle against my heart, if you would: seized against your will, you will elude the grasp like an essence—you will vanish ere I inhale your fragrance. Oh! come, Jane, come!"

As he said this, he released me from his clutch, and only looked at me. The look was far worse to resist than the frantic strain: only an idiot, however, would have succumbed now. I had dared and baffled his fury; I must elude his sorrow: I retired to the door.

"You are going, Jane?"

"I am going, sir."

"You are leaving me?"

"Yes."

"You will not come?—You will not be my comforter, my rescuer?—My deep love, my wild woe, my frantic prayer, are all nothing to you?"

What unutterable pathos was in his voice!

How hard it was to reiterate firmly, "I am going."

"Jane!"

"Mr. Rochester."

"Withdraw, then—I consent—but remember, you leave me here in anguish. Go up to your own room; think over all I have said, and, Jane, cast a glance on my sufferings—think of me."

He turned away; he threw himself on his face on the sofa. "Oh, Jane! my hope—my love—my life!" broke in anguish from his lips. Then came a deep, strong sob.

I had already gained the door: but, reader, I walked back—walked back as determinedly as I had retreated. I knelt down by him; I turned his face from the cushion to me; I kissed his cheek; I smoothed his hair with my hand.

"God bless you, my dear master," I said. "God keep you from harm and wrong—direct you, solace you—reward you well for your past kindness to me."

"Little Jane's love would have been my best reward," he answered: "without it, my heart is broken. But Jane will give me her love: yes—nobly, generously."

Up the blood rushed to his face; forth flashed the fire from his eyes; erect he sprang: he held his arms out; but I evaded the embrace, and at once quitted the room.

"Farewell!" was the cry of my heart, as

I left him. Despair added, — " Farewell for ever !"

*   *   *   *   *   *.

. That night I never thought to sleep : but a slumber fell on me as soon as I lay down in bed. I was transported in thought to the scenes of childhood : I dreamt I lay in the red-room at Gateshead ; that the night was dark, and my mind impressed with strange fears. The light that long ago had struck me into syncope, recalled in this vision, seemed glidingly to mount the wall, and tremblingly to pause in the centre of the obscured ceiling. I lifted up my head to look : the roof resolved to clouds, high and dim ; the gleam was such as the moon imparts to vapours she is about to sever. I watched her come— watched with the strangest anticipation ; as though some word of doom were to be written on her disk. She broke forth as never moon yet burst from cloud : a hand first penetrated the sable folds and waved them away ; then, not a moon, but a white human form shone in the azure, in-clining a glorious brow earthward. It gazed and gazed on me. It spoke, to my spirit : immeasure-ably distant was the tone, yet so near, it whispered in my heart—

" My daughter, flee temptation !"

" Mother, I will."

So I answered after I had waked from the trance-like dream. It was yet night, but July

nights are short: soon after midnight, dawn
comes. "It cannot be too early to commence the
task I have to fulfil," thought I. I rose: I was
dressed; for I had taken off nothing but my shoes.
I knew where to find in my drawers some linen,
a locket, a ring. In seeking these articles, I
encountered the beads of a pearl necklace Mr.
Rochester had forced me to accept a few days
ago. I left that; it was not mine: it was the
visionary bride's who had melted in air. The
other articles I made up in a parcel; my purse,
containing twenty shillings (it was all I had), I
put in my pocket: I tied on my straw bonnet,
pinned my shawl, took the parcel and my slippers,
which I would not put on yet, and stole from my
room.

"Farewell, kind Mrs. Fairfax!" I whispered,
as I glided past her door. "Farewell, my darling Adèle!" I said, as I glanced towards the
nursery. No thought could be admitted of
entering to embrace her. I had to deceive
a fine ear: for aught I knew, it might now be
listening.

I would have got past Mr. Rochester's chamber
without a pause; but my heart momentarily stop-
ping its beat at that threshold, my foot was forced
to stop also. No sleep was there: the inmate
was walking restlessly from wall to wall; and
again and again he sighed while I listened. There
was a heaven—a temporary heaven—in this room

for me, if I chose: I had but to go in and to say—

"Mr. Rochester, I will love you and live with you through life till death," and a fount of rapture would spring to my lips. I thought of this.

That kind master, who could not sleep now, was waiting with impatience for day. He would send for me in the morning: I should be gone. He would have me sought for: vainly. He would feel himself forsaken; his love rejected: he would suffer; perhaps grow desperate. I thought of this too. My hand moved towards the lock: I caught it back, and glided on.

Drearily I wound my way down stairs: I knew what I had to do, and I did it mechanically. I sought the key of the side-door in the kitchen; I sought, too, a phial of oil and a feather; I oiled the key and the lock. I got some water, I got some bread: for perhaps I should have to walk far; and my strength, sorely shaken of late, must not break down. All this I did without one sound. I opened the door, passed out, shut it softly. Dim dawn glimmered in the yard. The great gates were closed and locked; but a wicket in one of them was only latched. Through that I departed: it, too, I shut; and now I was out of Thornfield.

A mile off, beyond the fields, lay a road which stretched in the contrary direction to Millcote;

a road I had never travelled,.but often noticed, and wondered where it led : thither I bent my steps. No reflection was to be allowed now : not one glance was to be cast back ; not even one forward. Not one thought was to be given either to the past, or the future. The first was a page so heavenly sweet—so deadly sad—that to read one line of it would dissolve my courage and break down my energy. The last was an awful blank : something like the world when the deluge was gone by.

I skirted fields, and hedges, and lanes, till after sunrise. I believe it was a lovely summer morning : I know my shoes, which I had put on when I left the house, were soon wet with dew. But I looked neither to rising sun, nor smiling sky, nor wakening nature. He who is taken out to pass through a fair scene to the scaffold, thinks not of the flowers that smile on his road, but of the block and axe-edge ; of the disseverment of bone and vein ; of the grave gaping at the end : and I thought of drear flight and homeless wandering—and, oh! with agony I thought of what I left! I could not help it. I thought of him now—in his room—watching the sunrise ; hoping I should soon come to say I would stay with him, and be his. I longed to be his ; I panted to return : it was not too late ; I could yet spare him the bitter pang of bereavement. As yet my flight, I was sure, was undiscovered. I could go back

and be his comforter—his pride; his redeemer
from misery; perhaps from ruin. Oh, that fear
of his self-abandonment — far worse than my
abandonment—how it goaded me! It was a
barbed arrow-head in my breast: it tore me when
I tried to extract it; it sickened me when Remembrance thrust it further in. Birds began
singing in brake and copse: birds were faithful
to their mates; birds were emblems of love.
What was I? In the midst of my pain of heart,
and frantic effort of principle, I abhorred myself.
I had no solace from self-approbation: none even
from self-respect. I had injured—wounded—left
my master. I was hateful in my own eyes. Still
I could not turn, nor retrace one step. God
must have led me on. As to my own will or
conscience, impassioned grief had trampled one
and stifled the other. I was weeping wildly as
I walked along my solitary way: fast, fast I went
like one delirious. A weakness, beginning inwardly, extending to the limbs, seized me, and
I fell: I lay on the ground some minutes, pres-
sing my face to the wet turf. I had some fear—
or hope—that here I should die: but I was soon
up; crawling forwards on my hands and knees,
and then again raised to my feet—as eager and
as determined as ever to reach the road.

When I got there, I was forced to sit to rest
me under the hedge; and while I sat, I heard
wheels, and saw a coach come on. I stood up

and lifted my hand; it stopped. I asked where it was going: the driver named a place a long way off, and where I was sure Mr. Rochester had no connexions. I asked for what sum he would take me there; he said thirty shillings; I answered I had but twenty: well, he would try to make it do. He further gave me leave to get into the inside, as the vehicle was empty: I entered, was shut in, and it rolled on its way.

Gentle reader, may you never feel what I then felt! May your eyes never shed such stormy, scalding, heart-wrung tears as poured from mine. May you never appeal to Heaven in prayers so hopeless and so agonized as in that hour left my lips: for never may you, like me, dread to be the instrument of evil to what you wholly love.

CHAPTER II.

Two days are passed. It is a summer evening; the coachman has set me down at a place called Whitcross : he could take me no farther for the sum I had given, and I was not possessed of another shilling in the world. The coach is a mile off by this time ; I am alone. At this moment I discover that I forgot to take my parcel out of the pocket of the coach, where I had placed it for safety: there it remains, there it must remain ; and now I am absolutely destitute.

Whitcross is no town, nor even a hamlet ; it is but a stone pillar set up where four roads meet : white-washed, I suppose, to be more obvious at a distance and in darkness. Four arms spring from its summit : the nearest town to which these point is, according to the inscription, distant ten miles; the farthest, above twenty. From the well-known names of these towns I learn in what county I have lighted ; a north-midland shire, dusk with moorland, ridged with mountain : this

I see.   There are great moors behind and on
each hand of me; there are waves of mountains
far beyond that deep valley at my feet.   The
population here must be thin, and I see no pas-
sengers on these roads: they stretch out east,
west, north and south—white, broad, lonely; they
are all cut in the moor, and the heather grows
deep and wild to their very verge.   Yet a chance
traveller might pass by; and I wish no eye to see
me now: strangers would wonder what I am
doing, lingering here at the sign-post, evidently
objectless and lost.   I might be questioned: I
could give no answer but what would sound
incredible and excite suspicion.   Not a tie holds
me to human society at this moment—not a
charm or hope calls me where my fellow-creatures
are—none that saw me would have a kind thought
or a good wish for me.   I have no relative but the
universal mother, Nature: I will seek her breast
and ask repose.

I struck straight into the heath: I held on to a
hollow I saw deeply furrowing the brown moor-
side; I waded, knee-deep in its dark growth; I
turned with its turnings, and finding a moss-
blackened granite crag in a hidden angle, I sat
down under it.   High banks of moor were about
me; the crag protected my head: the sky was
over that.

Some time passed before I felt tranquil even
here: I had a vague dread that wild cattle might

ve near, or that some sportsman or poacher might discover me. If a gust of wind swept the waste, I looked up, fearing it was the rush of a bull; if a plover whistled, I imagined it a man. Finding my apprehensions unfounded, however, and calmed by the deep silence that reigned as evening declined to night-fall, I took confidence. As yet I had not thought; I had only listened, watched, dreaded: now I regained the faculty of reflection.

What was I to do? Where to go? Oh, intolerable questions, when I could do nothing and go nowhere!—when a long way must yet be measured by my weary, trembling limbs, before I could reach human habitation—when cold charity must be entreated before I could get a lodging: reluctant sympathy importuned; almost certain repulse incurred; before my tale could be listened to, or one of my wants relieved!

I touched the heath: it was dry, and yet warm with the heat of the summer day. I looked at the sky; it was pure: a kindly star twinkled just above the chasm ridge. The dew fell, but with propitious softness; no breeze whispered. Nature seemed to me benign and good: I thought she loved me, outcast as I was; and I, who from man could anticipate only mistrust, rejection, insult, clung to her with filial fondness. To night, at least, I would be her guest—as I was her child: my mother would lodge me without

money and without price. I had one morsel of
bread yet: the remnant of a roll I had bought in
a town we passed through at noon with a stray
penny — my last coin.   I saw ripe bilberries
gleaming here and there, like jet beads in the
heath: I gathered a handful and eat them with
the bread.   My hunger, sharp before, was, if not
satisfied, appeased by this hermit's meal.   I said
my evening prayers at its conclusion, and then
chose my couch.

Beside the crag, the heath was very deep :
when I lay down my feet were buried in it ; rising
high on each side, it left only a narrow space for
the night-air to invade.   I folded my shawl
double, and spread it over me for a coverlet; a
low, mossy swell was my pillow.   Thus lodged, I
was not, at least at the commencement of the
night, cold.

My rest might have been blissful enough, only
a sad heart broke it.   It plained of its gaping
wounds, its inward bleeding, its riven chords.
It trembled for Mr. Rochester and his doom: it
bemoaned him with bitter pity; it demanded him
with ceaseless longing ; and, impotent as a bird
with both wings broken, it still quivered its
shattered pinions in vain attempts to seek him.

Worn out with this torture of thought, I rose to
my knees.   Night was come, and her planets
were risen : a safe, still night; too serene for the
companionship of fear.   We know that God is

everywhere; but certainly we feel His presence most when His works are on the grandest scale spread before us: and it is in the unclouded night-sky, where His worlds wheel their silent course, that we read clearest His infinitude, His omnipotence, His omnipresence. I had risen to my knees to pray for Mr. Rochester. Looking up, I, with tear-dimmed eyes, saw the mighty milky-way. Remembering what it was—what countless systems there swept space like a soft trace of light—I felt the might and strength of God. Sure was I of His efficiency to save what He had made: convinced I grew that neither earth should perish, nor one of the souls it treasured. I turned my prayer to thanksgiving: the Source of Life was also the Saviour of Spirits. Mr. Rochester was safe: he was God's, and by God would he be guarded. I again nestled to the breast of the hill; and erelong, in sleep, forgot sorrow.

But next day, Want came to me, pale and bare. Long after the little birds had left their nests; long after bees had come in the sweet prime of day to gather the heath honey before the dew was dried—when the long morning shadows were curtailed, and the sun filled earth and sky—I got up, and I looked round me.

What a still, hot, perfect day! What a golden desert this spreading moor! Everywhere sunshine. I wished I could live in it and on it. I saw a lizard run over the crag; I saw a bee busy among the sweet bilberries. I would fain at the moment have become bee or lizard, that I might have found fitting nutriment, permanent shelter here. But I was a human being, and had a human being's wants : I must not linger where there was nothing to supply them. I rose; I looked back at the bed I had left. Hopeless of the future, I wished but this—that my Maker had that night thought good to require my soul of me while I slept; and that this weary frame, absolved by death from further conflict with fate, had now but to decay quietly, and mingle in peace with the soil of this wilderness. Life, however, was yet in my possession; with all its requirements, and pains, and responsibilities. The burden must be carried; the want provided for; the suffering endured; the responsibility fulfilled. I set out.

Whitcross regained, I followed a road which led from the sun, now fervent and high. By no other circumstance had I will to decide my choice. I walked a long time, and when I thought I had nearly done enough, and might conscientiously yield to the fatigue that almost overpowered me— might relax this forced action, and, sitting down on a stone I saw near, submit resistlessly to the apathy that clogged heart and limb—I heard a bell chime—a church bell.

I turned in the direction of the sound, and there, amongst the romantic hills, whose changes and aspect I had ceased to note an hour ago, I saw a hamlet and a spire. All the valley at my right hand was full of pasture-fields, and corn-fields, and wood; and a glittering stream ran zig-zag through the varied shades of green, the mellowing grain, the sombre wood-land, the clear and sunny lea. Recalled by the rumbling of wheels to the road before me, I saw a heavily-laden waggon labouring up the hill; and not far beyond were two cows and their drover. Human life and human labour were near. I must struggle on: strive to live and bend to toil like the rest.

About two o'clock, P. M., I entered the village. At the bottom of its one street, there was a little shop with some cakes of bread in the window. I coveted a cake of bread. With that refreshment I could perhaps regain a degree of energy; without it, it would be difficult to proceed. The wish to have some strength and some vigour returned to me as soon as I was amongst my fellow-beings. I felt it would be degrading to faint with hunger on the causeway of a hamlet. Had I nothing about me I could offer in exchange for one of these rolls? I considered. I had a small silk handkerchief tied round my throat; I had my gloves. I could hardly tell how men and women in extremities of destitution proceeded. I did not know whether either of these articles would be accepted: probably they would not; but I must try.

I entered the shop: a woman was there. Seeing a respectably-dressed person, a lady as she supposed, she came forward with civility. How could she serve me? I was seized with shame: my tongue would not utter the request I had prepared. I dared not offer her the half-worn gloves, the creased handkerchief: besides, I felt it would be absurd. I only begged permission to sit down a moment, as I was tired. Disappointed in the expectation of a customer, she coolly acceded to my request. She pointed to a seat; I sank into it. I felt sorely urged to weep; but conscious how unseasonable such a manifestation would be, I restrained it. Soon I asked her "if there were any dressmaker or plain-work-woman in the village?"

"Yes; two or three. Quite as many as there was employment for."

I reflected. I was driven to the point now. I was brought face to face with Necessity. I stood in the position of one without a resource: without a friend; without a coin. I must do something. What? I must apply somewhere. Where?

"Did she know of any place in the neighbourhood where a servant was wanted?"

"Nay; she couldn't say."

"What was the chief trade in this place? What did most of the people do?"

"Some were farm labourers; a good deal

worked at Mr. Oliver's needle-factory, and at the foundry."

"Did Mr. Oliver employ women?"

"Nay; it was men's work."

"And what do the women do?"

"I knaw n't," was the answer. "Some does one thing, and some another. Poor folk mun get on as they can."

She seemed to be tired of my questions: and, indeed, what claim had I to importune her? A neighbour or two came in; my chair was evidently wanted. I took leave.

I passed up the street, looking as I went at all the houses to the right hand and to the left: but I could discover no pretext, nor see an inducement, to enter any. I rambled round the hamlet, going sometimes to a little distance and returning again, for an hour or more. Much exhausted, and suffering greatly now for want of food, I turned aside into a lane and sat down under the hedge. Ere many minutes had elapsed, I was again on my feet, however, and again searching something—a resource, or at least an informant. A pretty little house stood at the top of the lane, with a garden before it; exquisitely neat, and brilliantly blooming. I stopped at it. What business had I to approach the white door, or touch the glittering knocker? In what way could it possibly be the interest of the inhabitants of that dwelling to serve me? Yet I drew near and knocked. A mild-looking, cleanly-attired young woman opened the door. In such a voice as might be expected from a hopeless heart and fainting frame — a voice wretchedly low and faltering — I asked if a servant was wanted here?

" No," said she ; " we do not keep a servant."

" Can you tell me where I could get employment of any kind," I continued. " I am a stranger, without acquaintance, in this place. I want some work : no matter what."

But it was not her business to think for me, or to seek a place for me : besides, in her eyes, how doubtful must have appeared my character, position, tale. She shook her head, she " was sorry she could give me no information," and the white door closed, quite gently and civilly : but it shut me out. If she had held it open a little longer, I believe I should have begged a piece of bread ; for I was now brought low.

I could not bear to return to the sordid village ; where, besides, no prospect of aid was visible. I should have longed rather to deviate to a wood I saw not far off, which appeared in its thick shade to offer inviting shelter ; but I was so sick, so weak, so gnawed with nature's cravings, instinct kept me roaming round abodes where there was a chance of food. Solitude would be no solitude—rest no rest—while the vulture, hunger, thus sunk beak and talons in my side.

I drew near houses; I left them, and came back again, and again I wandered away: always repelled by the consciousness of having no claim to ask—no right to expect interest in my isolated lot. Meantime, the afternoon advanced, while I thus wandered about like a lost and starving dog. In crossing a field, I saw the church-spire before me: I hastened towards it. Near the church-yard, and in the middle of a garden, stood a well-built though small house, which I had no doubt was the parsonage. I remembered that strangers who arrive at a place where they have no friends, and who want employment, sometimes apply to the clergyman for introduction and aid. It is the clergyman's function to help—at least with advice—those who wish to help themselves. I seemed to have something like a right to seek counsel here. Renewing then, my courage, and gathering my feeble remains of strength, I pushed on. I reached the house, and knocked at the kitchen-door. An old woman opened; I asked was this the parsonage?

" Yes."

" Was the clergyman in?"

" No."

" Would he be in soon?"

" No, he was gone from home."

" To a distance?"

" Not so far—happen three mile. He had been called away by the sudden death of his father: he was at Marsh End now, and would very likely stay there a fortnight longer."

" Was there any lady of the house?"

" Nay, there was naught but her, and she was housekeeper;" and of her, reader, I could not bear to ask the relief for want of which I was sinking: I could not yet beg; and again I crawled away.

Once more I took off my handkerchief—once more I thought of the cakes of bread in the little shop. Oh, for but a crust! for but one mouthful to allay the pang of famine! Instinctively I turned my face again to the village: I found the shop again, and I went in; and though others were there besides the woman, I ventured the request, " Would she give me a roll for this handkerchief?"

She looked at me with evident suspicion: " Nay, she never sold stuff i' that way."

Almost desperate, I asked for half a cake: she again refused. " How could she tell where I had got the handkerchief," she said.

" Would she take my gloves?"

" No; what could she do with them?"

Reader, it is not pleasant to dwell on these details. Some say there is enjoyment in looking back to painful experience past; but at this day I can scarcely bear to review the times to which I allude: the moral degradation, blent with the physical suffering, form too distressing a recollection ever to be willingly dwelt on. I blamed none of those who repulsed me. I felt it was what was to be expected, and what could not be helped: an ordinary beggar is frequently an object of suspicion; a well-dressed beggar inevitably so. To be sure, what I begged was employment: but whose business was it to provide me with employment? Not, certainly that of persons who saw me then for the first time, and who knew nothing about my character. And as to the woman who would not take my handkerchief in exchange for her bread, why, she was right; if the offer appeared to her sinister, or the exchange unprofitable. Let me condense now. I am sick of the subject.

A little before dark I passed a farm-house, at the open door of which the farmer was sitting, eating his supper of bread and cheese: I stopped and said:—

"Will you give me a piece of bread? for I am very hungry." He cast on me a glance of surprise; but without answering, he cut a thick slice from his loaf, and gave it to me. I imagine he did not think I was a beggar, but only an eccentric sort of lady who had taken a fancy to his brown loaf. As soon as I was out of sight of his house, I sat down and ate it.

I could not hope to get a lodging under a roof, and sought it in the wood I have before alluded to. But my night was wretched, my rest broken:

the ground was damp, the air cold : besides, in-
truders passed near me more than once, and I
had again and again to change my quarters : no
sense of safety or tranquillity befriended me.
Towards morning it rained ; the whole of the
following day was wet. Do not ask me, reader,
to give a minute account of that day : as before, I
sought work ; as before, I was repulsed ; as before, I
starved : but once did food pass my lips. At the
door of a cottage I saw a little girl about to
throw a mess of cold porridge into a pig-trough.
" Will you give me that ?" I asked.

She stared at me. " Mother !" she exclaimed ;
" there is a woman wants me to give her these
porridge."

" Well, lass," replied a voice within, " give it
her if she 's a beggar. T' pig doesn't want it."

The girl emptied the stiffened mould into my
hand, and I devoured it ravenously.

As the wet twilight deepened, I stopped in a
solitary bridle-path, which I had been pursuing an
hour or more.

" My strength is quite failing me," I said, in
soliloquy. " I feel I cannot go much further.
Shall I be an outcast again this night ? While
the rain descends so, must I lay my head on the
cold, drenched ground ? I fear I cannot do
otherwise : for who will receive me ? But it
will be very dreadful : with this feeling of hunger,
faintness, chill, and this sense of desolation—this

total prostration of hope. In all likelihood, though, I should die before morning. And why cannot I reconcile myself to the prospect of death? Why do I struggle to retain a valueless life? Because I know, or believe, Mr. Rochester is still living: and then, to die of want and cold, is a fate to which nature cannot submit passively. Oh, Providence! sustain me a little longer! Aid —direct me!"

My glazed eye wandered over the dim and misty landscape. I saw I had strayed far from the village: it was quite out of sight. The very cultivation surrounding it had disappeared. I had, by cross-ways and by-paths, once more drawn near the tract of moorland; and now, only a few fields, almost as wild and unproductive as the heath from which they were scarcely reclaimed, lay between me and the dusky hill.

"Well; I would rather die yonder than in a street, or on a frequented road," I reflected. "And far better that crows and ravens—if any ravens there be in these regions—should pick my flesh from my bones, than that they should be prisoned in a workhouse coffin, and moulder in a pauper's grave."

To the hill, then, I turned. I reached it. It remained now only to find a hollow where I could lie down, and feel at least hidden, if not secure: but all the surface of the waste looked level. It showed no variation but of tint: green, where rush and moss overgrew the marshes; black, where the dry soil bore only heath. Dark as it was getting, I could still see these changes; though but as mere alternations of light and shade: for colour had faded with the daylight.

My eye still roved over the sullen swell, and along the moor - edge, vanishing amidst the wildest scenery; when, at one dim point, far in among the marshes and the ridges, a light sprung up. " That is an *ignis-fatuus*," was my first thought; and I expected it would soon vanish. It burnt on, however, quite steadily; neither receding nor advancing. " Is it then a bonfire just kindled?" I questioned. I watched to see whether it would spread: but no; as it did not diminish, so it did not enlarge. " It may be a candle in a house," I then conjectured: " but if so, I can never reach it. It is much too far away: and were it within a yard of me, what would it avail? I should but knock at the door to have it shut in my face."

And I sank down where I stood, and hid my face against the ground. I lay still awhile: the night-wind swept over the hill and over me, and died moaning in the distance; the rain fell fast, wetting me afresh to the skin. Could I but have stiffened to the still frost—the friendly numbness of death—it might have pelted on: I should not have felt it; but my yet living flesh shuddered to its chilling influence. I rose ere long.

The light was yet there; shining dim, but constant, through the rain. I tried to walk again: I dragged my exhausted limbs slowly towards it. It led me aslant over the hill, through a wide bog; which would have been impassable in winter, and was splashy and shaking even now, in the height of summer. Here I fell twice; but as often I rose and rallied my faculties. This light was my forlorn hope: I must gain it.

Having crossed the marsh, I saw a trace of white over the moor. I approached it; it was a road or a track: it led straight up to the light, which now beamed from a sort of knoll, amidst a clump of trees—firs, apparently, from what I could distinguish of the character of their forms and foliage through the gloom. My star vanished as I drew near: some obstacle had intervened between me and it. I put out my hand to feel the dark mass before me: I discriminated the rough stones of a low wall — above it, something like palisades, and within, a high and prickly hedge. I groped on. Again a whitish object gleamed before me: it was a gate—a wicket; it moved on its hinges as I touched it. On each side stood a sable bush—holly or yew.

Entering the gate and passing the shrubs, the silhouette of a house rose to view; black, low, and rather long: but the guiding light shone nowhere. All was obscurity. Were the inmates retired to rest? I feared it must be so. In seeking the door, I turned an angle : there shot out the friendly gleam again, from the lozenged panes of a very small latticed window, within a foot of the ground; made still smaller by the growth of ivy or some other creeping plant, whose leaves clustered thick over the portion of the house wall in which it was set. The aperture was so screened and narrow, that curtain or shutter had been deemed unnecessary; and when I stooped down and put aside the spray of foliage shooting over it, I could see all within. I could see clearly a room with a sanded floor, clean scoured; a dresser of walnut, with pewter plates ranged in rows, reflecting the redness and radiance of a glowing peat-fire. I could see a clock, a white deal table, some chairs. The candle, whose ray had been my beacon, burnt on the table; and by its light an elderly woman, somewhat rough-looking, but scrupulously clean, like all about her, was knitting a stocking.

I noticed these objects cursorily only—in them there was nothing extraordinary. A group of more interest appeared near the hearth, sitting still amidst the rosy peace and warmth suffusing it. Two young, graceful women—ladies in every point—sat, one in a low rocking-chair, the other on a lower stool; both wore deep mourning of crape and bombazeen, which sombre garb singularly set off their very fair necks and faces : a large old pointer dog rested its massive head on the knee of one girl—in the lap of the other was cushioned a black cat.

A strange place was this humble kitchen for such occupants! Who were they? They could not be the daughters of the elderly person at the table; for she looked like a rustic, and they were all delicacy and cultivation. I had nowhere seen such faces as theirs: and yet, as I gazed on them, I seemed intimate with every lineament. I cannot call them handsome—they were too pale and grave for the word: as they each bent over a book, they looked thoughtful almost to severity. A stand between them supported a second candle and two great volumes, to which they frequently referred; comparing them seemingly with the smaller books they held in their hands, like people consulting a dictionary to aid them in the task of translation. This scene was as silent as if all the figures had been shadows, and the fire-lit apartment a picture: so hushed was it, I could hear the cinders fall from the grate, the clock tick in its obscure corner; and I even fancied I could distinguish the click-click of the woman's knitting-needles. When, therefore, a voice broke the strange stillness at last, it was audible enough to me.

"Listen, Diana," said one of the absorbed students; "Franz and old Daniel are together in the night-time, and Franz is telling a dream from which he has wakened in terror—listen!" And in a low voice she read something, of which not one word was intelligible to me; for it was in an unknown tongue—neither French nor Latin.

Whether it were Greek or German I could not tell.

"That is strong," she said, when she had finished: "I relish it." The other girl, who had lifted her head to listen to her sister, repeated, while she gazed at the fire, a line of what had been read. At a later day, I knew the language and the book; therefore I will here quote the line : though, when I first heard it, it was only like a stroke on sounding brass to me —conveying no meaning :

"'Da trat hervor Einer, anzusehen wie die Sternen Nacht.' Good! good!" she exclaimed, while her dark and deep eye sparkled. "There you have a dim and mighty archangel fitly set before you! The line is worth a hundred pages of fustian. 'Ich wäge die Gedanken in der Schale meines Zornes und die Werke mit dem Gewichte meines Grimms.' I like it !"

Both were again silent.

"Is there ony country where they talk i' that way?" asked the old woman, looking up from her knitting.

"Yes, Hannah—a far larger country than England ; where they talk in no other way."

"Well, for sure case, I knawn't how they can understand t' one t' other : and if either o' ye went there, ye could tell what they said, I guess?"

"We could probably tell something of what they said, but not all—for we are not as clever as you think us, Hannah. We don't speak German, and we cannot read it without a dictionary to help us."

"And what good does it do you?"

"We mean to teach it some time—or at least the elements, as they say; and then we shall get more money than we do now."

"Varry like: but give ower studying; ye've done enough for to-night."

"I think we have: at least, I'm tired. Mary, are you?"

"Mortally: after all, it's tough work fagging away at a language with no master but a lexicon.'

"It is: especially such a language as this crabbed but glorious Deutsch. I wonder when St. John will come home."

"Surely he will not be long now: it is just ten" (looking at a little gold watch she drew from her girdle). "It rains fast. Hannah, will you have the goodness to look at the fire in the parlour?"

The woman rose; she opened a door, through which I dimly saw a passage: soon I heard her stir a fire in an inner room; she presently came back.

"Ah, childer!" said she, "it fair troubles me to go into yond' room now: it looks so lonesome wi' the chair empty and set back in a corner."

She wiped her eyes with her apron: the two girls, grave before, looked sad now.

"But he is in a better place," continued Hannah: "we shouldn't wish him here again.'

And then, nobody need to have a quieter death no he had."

"You say he never mentioned us?" inquired one of the ladies.

"He hadn't time, bairn: he was gone in a minute—was your father. He had been a bit ailing like the day before, but naught to signify; and when Mr. St. John asked if he would like either o' ye to be sent for, he fair laughed at him. He began again with a bit of a heaviness in his head the next day—that is, a fortnight sin'—and he went to sleep and niver wakened: he wor a'most stark when your brother went into t' chamber and fand him. Ah, childer! that's t' last o' t' old stock —for ye and Mr. St. John is like of a different soart to them 'at's gone; for all your mother wor mich i' your way, and a'most as book-learned. She wor the pictur' o' ye, Mary: Diana is more like your father."

I thought them so similar I could not tell where the old servant (for such I now concluded her to be) saw the difference. Both were fair complexioned and slenderly made; both possessed faces full of distinction and intelligence. One, to be sure, had hair a shade darker than the other, and there was a difference in their style of wearing it: Mary's pale brown locks were parted and braided smooth; Diana's duskier tresses covered her neck with thick curls. The clock struck ten.

"Ye 'll want your supper, I 'm sure," observed Hannah; "and so will Mr. St. John when he comes in."

And she proceeded to prepare the meal. The ladies rose: they seemed about to withdraw to the parlour. Till this moment, I had been so intent on watching them, their appearance and conversation had excited in me so keen an interest, I had half-forgotten my own wretched position: now it recurred to me. More desolate, more desperate than ever, it seemed from contrast. And how impossible did it appear to touch the inmates of this house with concern on my behalf: to make them believe in the truth of my wants and woes—to induce them to vouchsafe a rest for my wanderings! As I groped out the door, and knocked at it hesitatingly, I felt that last idea to be indeed a mere chimera. Hannah opened.

"What do you want?" she inquired, in a voice of surprise, as she surveyed me by the light of the candle she held.

"May I speak to your mistresses?" I said.

"You had better tell me what you have to say to them. Where do you come from?"

"I am a stranger."

"What is your business here at this hour?"

"I want a night's shelter in an out-house or anywhere, and a morsel of bread to eat."

Distrust, the very feeling I dreaded, appeared in Hannah's face. "I 'll give you a piece of bread," she said, after a pause; "but we can't take in a vagrant to lodge. It isn't likely."

"Do let me speak to your mistresses."

"No; not I. What can they do for you? You should not be roving about now: it looks very ill."

"But where shall I go if you drive me away? What shall I do?"

"Oh, I'll warrant you know where to go, and what to do. Mind you don't do wrong, that's all. Here is a penny; now go——."

"A penny cannot feed me, and I have no strength to go farther. Don't shut the door!—oh, don't, for God's sake!"

"I must; the rain is driving in——."

"Tell the young ladies.—Let me see them—."

"Indeed I will not. You are not what you ought to be, or you wouldn't make such a noise. Move off!"

"But I must die if I am turned away."

"Not you. I'm feard you have some ill plans agate, that bring you about folk's houses at this time o' night. If you've any followers—housebreakers or such like—anywhere near, you may tell them we are not by ourselves in the house: we have a gentleman, and dogs, and guns." Here the honest but inflexible servant clapped the door to and bolted it within.

This was the climax. A pang of exquisite suffering—a throe of true despair—rent and heaved my heart. Worn out, indeed, I was : not another step could I stir. I sank on the wet door-step : I groaned—I wrung my hands—I wept in utter anguish. Oh, this spectre of death! Oh, this last hour, approaching in such horror! Alas, this isolation—this banishment from my kind! Not only the anchor of hope, but the footing of forti-tude was gone—at least for a moment : but the last I soon endeavoured to regain.

"I can but die," I said, "and I believe in God. Let me try to wait His will in silence."

These words I not only thought but uttered ; and thrusting back all my misery into my heart, I made an effort to compel it to remain there—dumb and still.

"All men must die," said a voice quite close at hand; "but all are not condemned to meet a lingering and premature doom, such as yours would be if you perished here of want."

"Who or what speaks?" I asked, terrified at the unexpected sound, and incapable now of deriving from any occurrence a hope of aid. A form was near—what form, the pitch-dark night' and my enfeebled vision prevented me from dis-tinguishing. With a loud, long knock, the new comer appealed to the door.

"Is it you, Mr. St. John?" cried Hannah.

"Yes—yes ; open quickly."

"Well, how wet and cold you must be, such a wild night as it is! Come in—your sisters are quite uneasy about you, and I believe there are bad folks about. There has been a beggar-woman —I declare she is not gone yet!—laid down there. Get up! for shame! Move off, I say!"

"Hush, Hannah! I have a word to say to the woman. You have done your duty in excluding, now let me do mine in admitting her. I was near, and listened to both you and her. I think this is a peculiar case—I must at least examine into it. Young woman, rise, and pass before me into the house."

With difficulty I obeyed him. Presently I stood within that clean, bright kitchen—on the very hearth—trembling, sickening; conscious of an aspect in the last degree ghastly, wild, and weatherbeaten. The two ladies, their brother, Mr. St. John, the old servant, were all gazing at me.

"St. John, who is it?" I heard one ask.

"I cannot tell: I found her at the door," was the reply.

"She does look white," said Hannah.

"As white as clay or death," was responded. "She will fall: let her sit."

And indeed my head swam: I dropped; but a chair received me. I still possessed my senses; though just now I could not speak.

"Perhaps a little water would restore her. Hannah, fetch some. But she is worn to nothing. How very thin, and how very bloodless!"

"A mere spectre!"

" Is she ill, or only famished ? "

" Famished, I think. Hannah, is that milk ? Give it me, and a piece of bread."

Diana (I knew her by the long curls which I saw drooping between me and the fire as she bent over me) broke some bread, dipped it in milk, and put it to my lips. Her face was near mine : I saw there was pity in it, and I felt sympathy in her hurried breathing. In her simple words, too, the same balm-like emotion spoke : " Try to eat."

" Yes—try," repeated Mary gently ; and Mary's hand removed my sodden bonnet and lifted my head. I tasted what they offered me : feebly at first, eagerly soon.

" Not too much at first—restrain her," said the brother ; "she has had enough." And he withdrew the cup of milk and the plate of bread.

" A little more, St. John—look at the avidity in her eyes."

" No more at present, sister. Try if she can speak now—ask her her name."

I felt I could speak, and I answered—" My name is Jane Elliott." Anxious as ever to avoid discovery, I had before resolved to assume an *alias*.

" And where do you live ? Where are your friends ? "

I was silent.

" Can we send for any one you know ? "

I shook my head.

" What account can you give of yourself ? "

Somehow, now that I had once crossed the threshold of this house, and once was brought face to face with its owners, I felt no longer outcast, vagrant, and disowned by the wide world. I dared to put off the mendicant—to resume my natural manner and character. I began once more to know myself; and when Mr. St. John demanded an account—which at present I was far too weak to render—I said, after a brief pause—

" Sir, I can give you no details to-night."

" But what, then," said he, " do you expect me to do for you ?"

" Nothing," I replied. My strength sufficed for but short answers. Diana took the word:

" Do you mean," she asked, " that we have now given you what aid you require; and that we may dismiss you to the moor and the rainy night?"

I looked at her. She had, I thought, a remarkable countenance; instinct both with power and goodness. I took sudden courage. Answering her compassionate gaze with a smile, I said: " I will trust you. If I were a masterless and stray dog, I know that you would not turn me from your hearth to-night : as it is, I really have no fear. Do with me and for me as you like; but excuse me from much discourse—my breath is short—I feel a spasm when I speak." All three surveyed me, and all three were silent.

" Hannah," said Mr. St. John, at last, " let her sit there at present, and ask her no questions; in ten minutes more, give her the remainder of that milk and bread. Mary and Diana, let us go into the parlour and talk the matter over."

They withdrew. Very soon one of the ladies returned—I could not tell which. A kind of pleasant stupor was stealing over me as I sat by the genial fire. In an under tone, she gave some directions to Hannah. Erelong, with the servant's aid, I contrived to mount a staircase: my dripping clothes were removed; soon a warm, dry bed received me. I thanked God—experienced amidst unutterable exhaustion a glow of grateful joy—and slept.

CHAPTER III.

THE recollection of about three days and nights succeeding this is very dim in my mind. I can recall some sensations felt in that interval; but few thoughts framed, and no actions performed. I knew I was in a small room, and in a narrow bed. To that bed I seemed to have grown: I lay on it motionless as a stone; and to have torn me from it would have been almost to kill me. I took no note of the lapse of time—of the change from morning to noon, from noon to evening. I observed when any one entered or left the apartment; I could even tell who they were; I could understand what was said when the speaker stood near me; but I could not answer: to open my lips or move my limbs was equally impossible. Hannah, the servant, was my most frequent visitor. Her coming disturbed me. I had a feeling that she wished me away; that she did not understand me or my circumstances;

that she was prejudiced against me. Diana and Mary appeared in the chamber once or twice a day. They would whisper sentences of this sort at my bed-side :—

"It is very well we took her in."

"Yes; she would certainly have been found dead at the door in the morning, had she been left out all night. I wonder what she has gone through?"

"Strange hardships, I imagine—poor, emaciated, pallid wanderer!"

"She is not an uneducated person, I should think, by her manner of speaking: her accent was quite pure; and the clothes she took off, though splashed and wet, were little worn, and fine."

"She has a peculiar face; fleshless and haggard as it is: I rather like it; and when in good health and animated, I can fancy her physiognomy would be agreeable."

Never once in their dialogues did I hear a syllable of regret at the hospitality they had extended to me; or of suspicion of, or aversion to, myself. I was comforted.

Mr. St. John came but once: he looked at me, and said my state of lethargy was the result of reaction from excessive and protracted fatigue. He pronounced it needless to send for a doctor: nature, he was sure, would manage best, left to

herself. He said every nerve had been over-
strained in some way, and the whole system must
sleep torpid awhile. There was no disease. He
imagined my recovery would be rapid enough
when once commenced. These opinions he delivered in few words, in a quiet, low voice; and
added, after a pause, in the tone of a man little
accustomed to expansive comment, "rather an
unusual physiognomy: certainly, not indicative
of vulgarity or degradation."

"Far otherwise," responded Diana. "To speak
truth, St. John, my heart rather warms to the
poor little soul. I wish we may be able to benefit her permanently."

"That is hardly likely," was the reply. "You
will find she is some young lady who has had a mis-
understanding with her friends, and has probably
injudiciously left them. We may, perhaps, succeed in restoring her to them, if she is not obstinate : but I trace lines of force in her face which
make me sceptical of her tractability." He stood
considering me some minutes; then added, "She
looks sensible, but not at all handsome."

"She is so ill, St. John."

"Ill or well, she would always be plain. The
grace and harmony of beauty are quite wanting in
those features."

On the third day, I was better; on the fourth,

I could speak, move, rise in bed, and turn. Hannah had brought me some gruel and dry toast, about, as I supposed, the dinner hour. I had eaten with relish: the food was good—void of the feverish flavour which had hitherto poisoned what I had swallowed. When she left me, I felt comparatively strong and revived; erelong satiety of repose, and desire for action stirred me. I wished to rise: but what could I put on? Only my damp and bemired apparel; in which I had slept on the ground and fallen in the marsh. I felt ashamed to appear before my benefactors so clad. I was spared the humiliation.

On a chair by the bedside were all my own things, clean and dry. My black silk frock hung against the wall. The traces of the bog were removed from it; the creases left by the wet, smoothed out: it was quite decent. My very shoes and stockings were purified and rendered presentable. There were the means of washing in the room, and a comb and brush to smooth my hair. After a weary process, and resting every five minutes, I succeeded in dressing myself. My clothes hung loose on me; for I was much wasted: but I covered deficiencies with a shawl, and once more, clean and respectable-looking—no speck of the dirt, no trace of the disorder I so hated, and which seemed so to degrade me, left—I crept

down a stone staircase, with the aid of the ban-
nisters, to a narrow, low passage, and found my
way presently to the kitchen.

It was full of the fragrance of new bread, and
the warmth of a generous fire. Hannah was
baking. Prejudices, it is well known, are most
difficult to eradicate from the heart whose soil has
never been loosened or fertilized by education:
they grow there, firm as weeds among stones.
Hannah had been cold and stiff, indeed, at the
first: latterly, she had begun to relent a little;
and when she saw me come in tidy and well-
dressed, she even smiled.

"What, you have got up?" she said. "You are
better, then. You may sit you down in my chair
on the hearthstone, if you will."

She pointed to the rocking chair: I took it.
She bustled about, examining me every now and
then with the corner of her eye. Turning to me,
as she took some loaves from the oven, she asked,
bluntly,—

"Did you ever go a-begging afore you came
here?"

I was indignant for a moment: but remembering that anger was out of the question, and that I
had indeed appeared as a beggar to her, I answered
quietly; but still not without a certain marked
firmness,—

' " You are mistaken, in supposing me a beggar.
I am no beggar; any more than yourself or your
young ladies."

After a pause, she said, " I dunnut understand
that: you 've like no house, nor no brass, I
guess?"

" The want of house or brass (by which I suppose you mean money) does not make a beggar in
your sense of the word."

" Are you book-learned?" she inquired, presently.

" Yes, very."

" But you 've never been to boarding-school?"

" I was at a boarding-school eight years."

She opened her eyes wide. " Whatever cannot
ye keep yourseln for, then?"

" I have kept myself; and, I trust, shall keep
myself again. What are you going to do with
these gooseberries?" I inquired, as she brought
out a basket of the fruit.

" Mak' em into pies."

" Give them to me and I 'll pick them."

" Nay; I dunnut want ye to do nought."

" But I must do something. Let me have
them."

She consented; and she even brought me a
clean towel to spread over my dress, " lest," as
she said, " I should mucky it."

"Ye 've not been used to sarvant's wark, I see by your hands," she remarked. "Happen ye 've been a dressmaker?"

"No, you are wrong. And now, never mind what I have been: don't trouble your head further about me; but tell me the name of the house where we are."

"Some calls it Marsh-End, and some calls it Moor House."

"And the gentleman who lives here is called Mr. St. John?"

"Nay; he doesn't live here: he is only staying awhile. When he is at home, he is in his own parish at Morton."

"That village a few miles off?"

"Aye."

"And what is he?"

"He is a parson."

I remembered the answer of the old housekeeper at the parsonage, when I had asked to see the clergyman. "This, then, was his father's residence?"

"Aye; old Mr. Rivers lived here, and his father, and grandfather, and gurt (great) grandfather afore him."

"The name, then, of that gentleman, is Mr. St. John Rivers?"

"Aye; St. John is like his kirstened name."

" And his sisters are called Diana and Mary Rivers ? "

" Yes."

" Their father is dead ? "

" Dead three weeks sin', of a stroke."

" They have no mother ? "

" The mistress has been dead this mony a year."

" Have you lived with the family long ? "

" I 've lived here thirty year. I nursed them all three."

" That proves you must have been an honest and faithful servant. I will say so much for you, though you have had the incivility to call me a beggar."

She again regarded me with a surprised stare. " I believe," she said, " I was quite mista'en in my thoughts of you : but there is so mony cheats goes about, you mun forgie me."

" And though," I continued, rather severely, " you wished to turn me from the door, on a night when you should not have shut out a dog."

" Well, it was hard : but what can a body do ? I thought more o' th' childer nor of mysel : poor things ! They 've like nobody to tak' care on 'em but me. I 'm like to look sharpish."

I maintained a grave silence for some minutes.

"You munnut think too hardly of me," she again remarked.

"But I do think hardly of you," I said; "and I'll tell you why—not so much because you refused to give me shelter, or regarded me as an impostor, as because you just now made it a species of reproach that I had no "brass" and no house. Some of the best people that ever lived have been as destitute as I am; and if you are a Christian, you ought not to consider poverty a crime."

"No more I ought," said she: "Mr. St. John tells me so too; and I see I wor wrang—but I've clear a different notion on you now to what I had. You look a raight down dacent little crater."

"That will do—I forgive you now. Shake hands."

She put her floury and horny hand into mine; another and heartier smile illumined her rough face: and from that moment we were friends.

Hannah was evidently fond of talking. While I picked the fruit, and she made the paste for the pies, she proceeded to give me sundry details about her deceased master and mistress, and "the childer," as she called the young people.

Old Mr. Rivers, she said, was a plain man enough; but a gentleman, and of as ancient a family as could be found. Marsh-End had belonged to the Rivers' ever since it was a house: and it was, she affirmed, "aboon two hundred year old—for all it looked but a small, humble place, naught to compare wi' Mr. Oliver's grand hall down i' Morton Vale. But she could remember Bill Oliver's father a journeyman needle-maker; and th' Rivers' wor gentry i' th' owd days o' th' Henrys, as onybody might see by looking into th' registers i' Morton Church vestry." Still, she allowed, "the owd maister was like other folk—naught mich out o' t' common way: stark mad o' shooting, and farming, and sich like." The mistress was different. She was a great reader, and studied a deal; and the "bairns" had taken after her. There was nothing like them in these parts, nor ever had been: they had liked learning, all three, almost from the time they could speak; and they had always been "of a mak' of their own." Mr. St. John, when he grew up, would go to college and be a parson; and the girls, as soon as they left school, would seek places as governesses: for they had told her their father had some years ago lost a great deal of money, by a man he had trusted turning bankrupt; and as he was now not rich enough to give them fortunes, they must provide for themselves. They had lived very little at home for a long while, and were only come now to stay a few weeks on account of their father's death: but they did so like Marsh-End and Morton, and all these moors and hills about. They had been in London, and many other grand towns; but they always said there was no place like home: and then they were so agreeable with each other— never fell out nor "threaped." She did not know where there was such a family for being united.

Having finished my task of gooseberry picking, I asked where the two ladies and their brother were now.

" Gone over to Morton for a walk; but they would be back in half an hour to tea."

They returned within the time Hannah had allotted them: they entered by the kitchen door. Mr. St. John, when he saw me, merely bowed and passed through; the two ladies stopped: Mary, in a few words, kindly and calmly expressed the pleasure she felt in seeing me well enough to be able to come down; Diana took my hand: she shook her head at me.

" You should have waited for my leave to descend," she said. " You still look very pale— and so thin! Poor child!—poor girl!"

Diana had a voice toned, to my ear, like the cooing of a dove. She possessed eyes whose gaze I delighted to encounter. Her whole face seemed to me full of charm. Mary's countenance was equally intelligent—her features equally pretty: but her expression was more reserved; and her manners, though gentle, more distant. Diana looked and spoke with a certain authority: she had a will evidently. It was my nature to feel pleasure in yielding to an authority supported like hers; and to bend, where my conscience and self-respect permitted, to an active will.

" And what business have you here ?" she continued. " It is not your place. Mary and I sit in the kitchen sometimes, because at home we like to be free, even to license—but you are a visitor, and must go into the parlour."

" I am very well here."

" Not at all—with Hannah bustling about and covering you with flour."

" Besides, the fire is too hot for you," interposed Mary.

" To be sure," added her sister. " Come, you must be obedient." And still holding my hand, she made me rise, and led me into the inner room.

" Sit there," she said, placing me on the sofa, " while we take our things off and get the tea ready: it is another privilege we exercise in our little moorland home—to prepare our own meals when we are so inclined; or when Hannah is baking, brewing, washing, or ironing."

She closed the door, leaving me solus with Mr. St. John, who sat opposite; a book or newspaper in his hand. I examined, first, the parlour, and then its occupant.

The parlour was rather a small room, very plainly furnished; yet comfortable, because clean and neat. The old-fashioned chairs were very bright, and the walnut-wood table was like a looking-glass. A few strange, antique portraits of the men and women of other days decorated the stained walls; a cupboard with glass doors contained some books and an ancient set of china. There was no superfluous ornament in the room— not one modern piece of furniture, save a brace of work-boxes and a lady's desk in rosewood, which stood on a side-table : every thing—including the carpet and curtains—looked at once well worn and well saved.

Mr. St. John—sitting as still as one of the dusky pictures on the walls; keeping his eyes fixed on the page he perused, and his lips mutely sealed—was easy enough to examine. Had he been a statue instead of a man, he could not have been easier. He was young—perhaps from twenty-eight to thirty—tall, slender; his face riveted the eye : it was like a Greek face, very pure in outline; quite a straight, classic nose ; quite an Athenian mouth and chin. It is seldom, indeed, an English face comes so near the antique models as did his. He might well be a little shocked at the irregularity of my lineaments, his own being so harmonious. His eyes were large and blue, with brown lashes; his high forehead, colourless as ivory, was partially streaked over by careless locks of fair hair.

This is a gentle delineation, is it not, reader? Yet he whom it describes scarcely impressed one with the idea of a gentle, a yielding, an impressible, or even of a placid nature. Quiescent as he now sat, there was something about his nostril, his mouth, his brow, which, to my perceptions, indicated elements within either restless, or hard, or eager. He did not speak to me one word, nor even direct to me one glance, till his sisters returned. Diana, as she passed in and out, in the course of preparing tea, brought me a little cake, baked on the top of the oven.

" Eat that now," she said: " you must be hungry. Hannah says you have had nothing but some gruel since breakfast."

I did not refuse it, for my appetite was awakened and keen. Mr. Rivers now closed his book, approached the table, and, as he took a seat, fixed his blue, pictorial-looking eyes full on me. There was an unceremonious directness, a searching, decided steadfastness in his gaze now, which told that intention, and not diffidence, had hitherto kept it averted from the stranger.

" You are very hungry," he said.

" I am, sir.". It is my way—it always was my way, by instinct—ever to meet the brief with brevity, the direct with plainness.

" It is well for you that a low fever has forced you to abstain for the last three days : there would have been danger in yielding to the cravings of your appetite at first. Now you may eat; though still not immoderately."

" I trust I shall not eat long at your expense, sir," was my very clumsily-contrived, unpolished answer.

" No," he said, coolly : " when you have indicated to us the residence of your friends, we can write to them, and you may be restored to home."

" That, I must plainly tell you, it is out of my power to do; being absolutely without home and friends."

The three looked at me : but not distrustfully. I felt there was no suspicion in their glances : there was more of curiosity. I speak particularly of the young ladies. St. John's eyes, though clear enough in a literal sense, in a figurative one were difficult to fathom. He seemed to use them rather as instruments to search other people's thoughts, than as agents to reveal his own: the which combination of keenness and reserve was considerably more calculated to embarrass than to encourage.

"Do you mean to say," he asked, "that you are completely isolated from every connection?"

"I do. Not a tie links me to any living thing: not a claim do I possess to admittance under any roof in England."

"A most singular position at your age!"

Here I saw his glance directed to my hands, which were folded on the table before me. I wondered what he sought there: his words soon explained the quest.

"You have never been married? You are a spinster?"

Diana laughed. "Why, she can't be above seventeen or eighteen years old, St. John," said she.

"I am near nineteen: but I am not married. No."

I felt a burning glow mount to my face; for bitter and agitating recollections were awakened by the allusion to marriage. They all saw the embarrassment, and the emotion. Diana and Mary relieved me by turning their eyes elsewhere than to my crimsoned visage; but the colder and sterner brother continued to gaze, till the trouble he had excited forced out tears as well as colour.

" Where did you last reside ?" he now asked.

" You are too inquisitive, St. John," murmured Mary, in a low voice : but he leaned over the table and required an answer, by a second firm and piercing look.

" The name of the place where, and of the person with whom I lived, is my secret," I replied, concisely.

" Which, if you like, you have, in my opinion, a right to keep, both from St. John and every other questioner," remarked Diana.

" Yet if I know nothing about you or your history, I cannot help you," he said. " And you need help : do you not ?"

" I need it, and I seek it; so far, sir, that some true philanthropist will put me in the way of getting work which I can do, and the remuneration for which will keep me : if but in the barest necessaries of life."

" I know not whether I am a true philanthropist; yet I am willing to aid you to the utmost of my power, in a purpose so honest. First, then, tell me what you have been accustomed to do, and what you *can* do."

I had now swallowed my tea. I was mightily refreshed by the beverage; as much so as a giant with wine : it gave new tone to my unstrung nerves, and enabled me to address this penetrating young judge steadily.

"Mr. Rivers," I said, turning to him, and looking at him as he looked at me, openly and without diffidence, "you and your sisters have done me a great service—the greatest man can do his fellow-being: you have rescued me, by your noble hospitality, from death. This benefit conferred gives you an unlimited claim on my gratitude; and a claim, to a certain extent, on my confidence. I will tell you as much of the history of the wanderer you have harboured, as I can tell without compromising my own peace of mind—my own security, moral and physical, and that of others.

"I am an orphan; the daughter of a clergy-man. My parents died before I could know them. I was brought up a dependent; educated in a charitable institution. I will even tell you the name of the establishment, where I passed six years as a pupil, and two as a teacher—Lowood Orphan Asylum, —— shire: you will have heard of it, Mr. Rivers?—the Rev. Robert Brocklehurst is the treasurer."

"I have heard of Mr. Brocklehurst, and I have seen the school."

"I left Lowood nearly a year since to become a private governess. I obtained a good situation, and was happy. This place I was obliged to leave

four days before I came here.   The reason of my
departure I cannot and ought not to explain: it
would be useless—dangerous; and would sound
incredible.   No blame attached to me: I am as
free from culpability as any one of you three.
Miserable I am, and must be for a time; for the
catastrophe which drove me from a house I had
found a paradise was of a strange and direful
nature.   I observed but two points in planning
my departure—speed, secrecy: to secure these, I
had to leave behind me every thing I possessed,
except a small parcel; which, in my hurry and
trouble of mind, I forgot to take out of the coach
that brought me to Whitcross.   To this neighbour-
nood, then, I came, quite destitute.   I slept two
nights in the open air, and wandered about two
days without crossing a threshold: but twice in
that space of time did I taste food; and it was
when brought by hunger, exhaustion, and despair,
almost to the last gasp, that you, Mr. Rivers, for-
bad me to perish of want at your door, and took
me under the shelter of your roof.   I know all
your sisters have done for me since—for I have not
been insensible during my seeming torpor—and I
owe to their spontaneous, genuine, genial compassion, as large a debt as to your evangelical charity."

   " Don't make her talk any more now, St. John,"
said Diana as I paused ; " she is evidently not yet

fit for excitement. Come to the sofa, and sit down now, Miss Elliott."

I gave an involuntary half-start at hearing the *alias:* I had forgotten my new name. Mr. Rivers, whom nothing seemed to escape, noticed it at once.

"You said your name was Jane Elliott?" he observed.

"I did say so; and it is the name by which I think it expedient to be called at present: but it is not my real name, and when I hear it, it sounds strange to me."

"Your real name you will not give?"

"No: I fear discovery above all things; and whatever disclosure would lead to it I avoid."

"You are quite right, I am sure," said Diana. "Now, do, brother, let her be at peace a while."

But when St. John had mused a few moments, he recommenced, as imperturbably, and with as much acumen as ever.

"You would not like to be long dependent on our hospitality—you would wish, I see, to dispense as soon as may be with my sisters' compassion; and, above all, with my *charity* (I am quite sensible of the distinction drawn, nor do I resent it—it is just): you desire to be independent of us?"

"I do: I have already said so. Show me how to work, or how to seek work: that is all I now ask; then let me go, if it be but to the meanest cottage—but *till then*, allow me to stay here : I dread another essay of the horrors of homeless destitution."

"Indeed, you *shall* stay here," said Diana, putting her white hand on my head. "You *shall*," repeated Mary, in the tone of undemonstrative sincerity, which seemed natural to her.

"My sisters, you see, have a pleasure in keeping you," said Mr. St. John," as they would have a pleasure in keeping and cherishing a half-frozen bird, some wintry wind might have driven through their casement. *I* feel more inclination to put you in the way of keeping yourself; and shall endeavour to do so : but observe, my sphere is narrow. I am but the incumbent of a poor country parish : my aid must be of the humblest sort. And if you are inclined to despise the day of small things, seek some more efficient succour than such as I can offer."

"She has already said that she is willing to do anything honest she *can* do," answered Diana, for me; " and you know, St. John, she has no choice of helpers : she is forced to put up with such crusty people as you."

"I will be a dressmaker: I will be a plain-work-woman; I will be a servant, a nurse-girl, if I can be no better," I answered.

" Right," said Mr. St. John, quite coolly. " If

such is your spirit, I promise to aid you; in my own time and way."

He now resumed the book with which he had been occupied before tea. I soon withdrew; for I had talked as much, and sat up as long, as my present strength would permit.

CHAPTER IV.

THE more I knew of the inmates of Moor-House, the better I liked them. In a few days I had so far recovered my health that I could sit up all day, and walk out sometimes. I could join with Diana and Mary in all their occupations; converse with them as much as they wished, and aid them when and where they would allow me. There was a reviving pleasure in this intercourse, of a kind now tasted by me for the first time—the pleasure arising from perfect congeniality of tastes, sentiments, and principles.

I liked to read what they liked to read : what they enjoyed, delighted me; what they approved, I reverenced. They loved their sequestered home. I, too, in the gray, small, antique structure, with its low roof, its latticed casements, its mouldering walls, its avenue of aged firs—all grown aslant under the stress of mountain winds; its garden, dark with yew and holly—and where no flowers but of the hardiest species would bloom—found a charm, both potent and permanent. They clung to the purple moors behind and around their dwelling—to the hollow vale into which the pebbly bridle-path leading from their gate descended; and which wound between fern-banks first, and then amongst a few of the wildest little pasture-fields that ever bordered a wilderness of heath, or gave sustenance to a flock of gray moorland sheep, with their little mossy-faced lambs:—they clung to this scene, I say, with a perfect enthusiasm of attachment. I could comprehend the feeling, and share both its strength and truth. I saw the fascination of the locality. I felt the consecration of its loneliness: my eye feasted on the outline of swell and sweep—on the wild colouring communicated to ridge and dell, by moss, by heath-bell, by flower-sprinkled turf, by brilliant bracken, and mellow granite crag. These details were just to me what they were to them—so many pure and sweet sources of pleasure. The strong blast and the soft breeze; the rough and the halcyon day; the hours of sunrise and sunset; the moonlight and the clouded night, developed for me, in these regions, the same attraction as for them—wound round my faculties the same spell that entranced theirs.

In-doors we agreed equally well. They were

both more accomplished and better read than I
was : but with eagerness I followed in the path of
knowledge they had trodden before me. I devoured the books they lent me : then it was full
satisfaction to discuss with them in the evening
what I had perused during the day. Thought
fitted thought; opinion met opinion : we coincided, in short, perfectly.

If in our trio there was a superior and a leader,
it was Diana. Physically, she far excelled me :
she was handsome; she was vigorous. In her
animal spirits, there was an affluence of life, and
certainty of flow, such as excited my wonder,
while it baffled my comprehension. I could talk
a while when the evening commenced : but the
first gush of vivacity and fluency gone, I was fain
to sit on a stool at Diana's feet, to rest my head
on her knee, and listen alternately to her and
Mary; while they sounded thoroughly the topic
on which I had but touched. Diana offered to
teach me German. I liked to learn of her : I
saw the part of instructress pleased and suited
her; that of scholar pleased and suited me no
less. Our natures dovetailed : mutual affection
—of the strongest kind—was the result. They
discovered I could draw : their pencils and colour-
boxes were immediately at my service. My skill,
greater in this one point than theirs, surprised

and charmed them. Mary would sit and watch me by the hour together: then she would take lessons; and a docile, intelligent, assiduous pupil, she made. Thus occupied, and mutually entertained, days passed like hours, and weeks like days.

As to Mr. St. John, the intimacy which had arisen so naturally and rapidly between me and his sisters, did not extend to him. One reason of the distance yet observed between us was, that he was comparatively seldom at home: a large proportion of his time appeared devoted to visiting the sick and poor among the scattered population of his parish.

No weather seemed to hinder him in these pastoral excursions: rain or fair, he would, when his hours of morning study were over, take his hat, and, followed by his father's old pointer, Carlo, go out on his mission of love, or duty—I scarcely know in which light he regarded it. Sometimes, when the day was very unfavourable, his sisters would expostulate. He would then say, with a peculiar smile, more solemn than cheerful,—

"And if I let a gust of wind or a sprinkling of rain turn me aside from these easy tasks, what preparation would such sloth be for the future I propose to myself?"

Diana and Mary's general answer to this ques_

tion was a sigh, and some minutes of apparently mournful meditation.

But besides his frequent absences, there was another barrier to friendship with him : he seemed of a reserved, an abstracted, and even of a brooding nature. Zealous in his ministerial labours, blameless in his life and habits, he yet did not appear to enjoy that mental serenity, that inward content, which should be the reward of every sincere Christian and practical philanthropist. Often, of an evening, when he sat at the window, his desk and papers before him, he would cease reading or writing, rest his chin on his hand, and deliver himself up to I know not what course of thought : but that it was perturbed and exciting might be seen in the frequent flash and changeful dilation of his eye.

I think, moreover, that Nature was not to him that treasury of delight it was to his sisters. He expressed once, and but once in my hearing, a strong sense of the rugged charm of the hills, and an inborn affection for the dark roof and hoary walls he called his home : but there was more of gloom than pleasure in the tone and words in which the sentiment was manifested ; and never did he seem to roam the moors for the sake of their soothing silence—never seek out or dwell upon the thousand peaceful delights they could yield.

Incommunicative as he was, some time elapsed before I had an opportunity of gauging his mind. I first got an idea of its calibre when I heard him preach in his own church at Morton. I wish I could describe that sermon: but it is past my power. I cannot even render faithfully the effect it produced on me.

It began calm—and indeed, as far as delivery and pitch of voice went, it was calm to the end: an earnestly felt, yet strictly restrained zeal breathed soon in the distinct accents, and prompted the nervous language. This grew to force—compressed, condensed, controlled. The heart was thrilled, the mind astonished, by the power of the preacher: neither were softened. Throughout there was a strange bitterness; an absence of consolatory gentleness: stern allusions to Calvinistic doctrines—election, predestination, reprobation— were frequent; and each reference to these points sounded like a sentence pronounced for doom. When he had done, instead of feeling better, calmer, more enlightened by his discourse, I experienced an inexpressible sadness; for it seemed to me—I know not whether equally so to others— that the eloquence to which I had been listening had sprung from a depth where lay turbid dregs of disappointment—where moved troubling impulses of insatiate yearnings and disquieting aspirations.

I was sure St. John Rivers—pure-lived, conscientious, zealous as he was—had not yet found that peace of God which passeth all understanding: he had no more found it, I thought, than had I; with my concealed and racking regrets for my broken idol and lost elysium—regrets to which I have latterly avoided referring ; but which possessed me and tyrannized over me ruthlessly.

Meantime, a month was gone. Diana and Mary were soon to leave Moor-House, and return to the far different life and scene which awaited them, as governesses in a large, fashionable, south-of-England city; where each held a situation in families, by whose wealthy and haughty members they were regarded only as humble dependants, and who neither knew nor sought one of their innate excellences, and appreciated only their acquired accomplishments as they appreciated the skill of their cook, or the taste of their waiting woman. Mr. St. John had said nothing to me yet about the employment he had promised to obtain for me : yet it became urgent that I should have a vocation of some kind. One morning, being left alone with him a few minutes in the parlour, I ventured to approach the window-recess—which his table, chair, and desk consecrated as a kind of study—and I was going to speak; though not very well knowing in what words to frame my inquiry—for it is at all times difficult to break the ice of reserve glassing over such natures as his—when he saved me the trouble, by being the first to commence a dialogue.

Looking up as I drew near—" You have a question to ask of me?" he said.

" Yes; I wish to know whether you have heard of any service I can offer myself to undertake."

" I found or devised something for you three weeks ago; but as you seemed both useful and happy here—as my sisters had evidently become attached to you, and your society gave them unusual pleasure—I deemed it inexpedient to break in on your mutual comfort, till their approaching departure from Marsh-End should render yours necessary."

" And they will go in three days now?" I said.

" Yes; and when they go, I shall return to the parsonage at Morton: Hannah will accompany me; and this old house will be shut up."

I waited a few moments, expecting he would go on with the subject first broached; but he seemed to have entered another train of reflection: his look denoted abstraction from me and my business. I was obliged to recall him to a theme which was of necessity one of close and anxious interest to me.

" What is the employment you had in view

Mr. Rivers?   I hope this delay will not have increased the difficulty of securing it."

" Oh, no; since it is an employment which depends only on me to give, and you to accept."

He again paused: there seemed a reluctance to continue.   I grew impatient: a restless movement or two, and an eager and exacting glance fastened on his face, conveyed the feeling to him as effectually as words could have done, and with less trouble.

" You need be in no hurry to hear," he said: " let me frankly tell you, I have nothing eligible or profitable to suggest.   Before I explain, recall, if you please, my notice, clearly given, that if I helped you, it must be as the blind man would help the lame.   I am poor; for I find that, when I have paid my father's debts, all the patrimony remaining to me will be this crumbling grange, the row of scathed firs behind, and the patch of moorish soil, with the yew-trees and holly-bushes in front.   I am obscure: Rivers is an old name; but of the three sole descendants of the race, two earn the dependant's crust among strangers, and the third considers himself an alien from his native country —not only for life, but in death.   Yes, and deems, and is bound to deem himself honoured by the lot; and aspires but after the day when the cross of separation from fleshly ties shall be laid on his

shoulders, and when the Head of that church-
militant of whose humblest members he is one,
shall give the word, ' Rise, follow me!' "

St. John said these words as he pronounced his
sermons, with a quiet, deep voice; with an unflushed
cheek, and a coruscating radiance of glance. He
resumed :—

" And since I am myself poor and obscure, I can
offer you but a service of poverty and obscurity.
You may even think it degrading—for I see now
your habits have been what the world calls refined :
your tastes lean to the ideal; and your society has
at least been amongst the educated—but *I* consider that no service degrades which can better our
race. I hold that the more arid and unreclaimed
the soil where the Christian labourer's task of til-
lage is appointed him—the scantier the meed his
toil brings—the higher the honour. His, under
such circumstances, is the destiny of the pioneer :
and the first pioneers of the Gospel were the
Apostles—their captain was Jesus, the Redeemer,
himself."

" Well?" I said, as he again paused—" proceed."

He looked at me before he proceeded: indeed,
he seemed leisurely to read my face, as if its
features and lines were characters on a page. The
conclusions drawn from this scrutiny he partially
expressed in his succeeding observations.

" I believe you will accept the post I offer you," said he; "and hold it for a while : not permanently, though: any more than I could permanently keep the narrow and narrowing—the tranquil, hidden office of English country incumbent: for in your nature is an alloy as detrimental to repose as that in mine; though of a different kind."

" Do explain ?" I urged, when he halted once more.

" I will; and you shall hear how poor the proposal is—how trivial—how cramping. I shall not stay long at Morton, now that my father is dead, and that I am my own master. I shall leave the place probably in the course of a twelvemonth : but while I *do* stay, I will exert myself to the utmost for its improvement. Morton, when I came to it two years ago, had no school : the children of the poor were excluded from every hope of progress. I established one for boys: I mean now to open a second school for girls. I have hired a building for the purpose, with a cottage of two rooms attached to it for the mistress's house. Her salary will be thirty pounds a year: her house is already furnished, very simply, but sufficiently, by the kindness of a lady, Miss Oliver; the only daughter of the sole rich man in my parish—Mr. Oliver, the proprietor of a needle-factory and iron-foundry in the valley. The same lady pays for the education and clothing of an orphan from the workhouse; on condition that she shall aid the mistress in such menial offices connected with her own house and the school, as her occupation of teaching will prevent her having time to discharge in person. Will you be this mistress?"

He put the question rather hurriedly; he seemed half to expect an indignant, or at least a disdainful rejection of the offer: not knowing all my thoughts and feelings, though guessing some, he could not tell in what light the lot would appear to me. In truth it was humble—but then it was sheltered, and I wanted a safe asylum: it was plodding—but then, compared with that of a governess in a rich house, it was independent; and the fear of servitude with strangers entered my soul like iron: it was not ignoble—not unworthy—not mentally degrading. I made my decision.

"I thank you for the proposal, Mr. Rivers; and I accept it with all my heart."

"But you comprehend me?" he said. "It is a village-school: your scholars will be only poor girls—cottagers' children—at the best, farmers' daughters. Knitting, sewing, reading, writing, cyphering, will be all you will have to teach. What will you do with your accomplishments? What, with the largest portion of your mind—sentiments—tastes?"

"Save them till they are wanted. They will keep."

"You know what you undertake, then?"

"I do."

He now smiled: and not a bitter or a sad smile; but one well pleased and deeply gratified.

"And when will you commence the exercise of your function?"

"I will go to my house to-morrow; and open the school, if you like, next week."

"Very well: so be it."

He rose and walked through the room. Standing still, he again looked at me. He shook his head.

"What do you disapprove of, Mr. Rivers?" I asked.

"You will not stay at Morton long: no, no!"

"Why? What is your reason for saying so?"

"I read it in your eye: it is not of that description which promises the maintenance of an even tenor in life."

"I am not ambitious."

He started at the word "ambitious." He repeated, "No. What made you think of ambition? Who is ambitious? I know I am: but how did you find it out?"

"I was speaking of myself."

"Well, if you are not ambitious, you are——."
He paused.

"What?"

"I was going to say, impassioned: but perhaps you would have misunderstood the word, and been displeased. I mean, that human affections and sympathies have a most powerful hold on you. I am sure you cannot long be content to pass your leisure in solitude, and to devote your working hours to a monotonous labour wholly void of stimulus; any more than I can be content," he added, with emphasis, "to live here buried in morass, pent in with mountain—my nature, that God gave me, contravened; my faculties, heaven-bestowed, paralyzed—made useless. You hear now how I contradict myself. I, who preached contentment with a humble lot, and justified the vocation even of hewers of wood, and drawers of water, in God's service—I, his ordained minister, almost rave in my restlessness. Well, propensities and principles must be reconciled by some means."

He left the room. In this brief hour I had learnt more of him than in the whole previous month: yet still he puzzled me.

Diana and Mary Rivers became more sad and silent as the day approached for leaving their brother, and their home. They both tried

to appear as usual; but the sorrow they had to
struggle against was one that could not be entirely
conquered or concealed. Diana intimated that
this would be a different parting from any they
had ever yet known. It would probably, as far as
St. John was concerned, be a parting for years:
it might be a parting for life.

"He will sacrifice all to his long-framed re-
solves," she said: "natural affection and feelings
more potent still. St. John looks quiet, Jane,
but he hides a fever in his vitals. You would
think him gentle, yet in some things he is inexorable as death; and the worst of it is, my
conscience will hardly permit me to dissuade him
from his severe decision: certainly, I cannot
for a moment blame him for it. It is right, noble,
Christian: yet it breaks my heart." And the
tears gushed to her fine eyes. Mary bent her
head low over her work.

"We are now without father: we shall soon be
without home and brother," she murmured.

At that moment a little accident supervened,
which seemed decreed by fate, purposely to prove
the truth of the adage, that "misfortunes never
come singly;" and to add to their distresses the
vexing one of the slip between the cup and the
lip. St. John passed the window reading a letter.
He entered.

" Our uncle John is dead," said he.

Both the sisters seemed struck : not shocked or appalled : the tidings appeared in their eyes rather momentous than afflicting.

" Dead ?" repeated Diana.

" Yes."

She riveted a searching gaze on her brother's face. " And what then ?" she demanded, in a low voice.

" What then, Die?" he replied, maintaining a marble immobility of feature. " What then? Why—nothing. Read."

He threw the letter into her lap. She glanced over it, and handed it to Mary. Mary perused it in silence, and returned it to her brother. All three looked at each other, and all three smiled—a dreary, pensive smile enough.

" Amen ! We can yet live," said Diana, at last.

" At any rate, it makes us no worse off than we were before," remarked Mary.

" Only it forces rather strongly on the mind the picture of what *might have been*," said Mr. Rivers ; " and contrasts it somewhat too vividly with what *is*."

He folded the letter, locked it in his desk, and again went out.

For some minutes no one spoke. Diana then turned to me.

" Jane, you will wonder at us and our mys-

teries," she said; " and think us hard-hearted
beings not to be more moved at the death of so
near a relation as an uncle : but we have never
seen him or known him. He was my mother's
brother. My father and he quarrelled long ago.
It was by his advice that my father risked most
of his property in the speculation that ruined him.
Mutual recriminations passed between them : they
parted in anger, and were never reconciled. My
uncle engaged afterwards in more prosperous
undertakings : it appears he realised a fortune of
twenty thousand pounds. He was never married,
and had no near kindred but ourselves, and one
other person, not more closely related than we.
My father always cherished the idea that he would
atone for his error, by leaving his possessions to
us : that letter informs us that he has bequeathed
every penny to the other relation ; with the exception of thirty guineas, to be divided between
St. John, Diana, and Mary Rivers, for the purchase of three mourning rings. He had a right,
of course, to do as he pleased : and yet a mo-
mentary damp is cast on the spirits by the receipt
of such news. Mary and I would have esteemed
ourselves rich with a thousand pounds each ; and
to St. John such a sum would have been valuable,
for the good it would have enabled him to do."

This explanation given, the subject was dropped,

and no further reference made to it, by either Mr. Rivers or his sisters. The next day, I left Marsh End for Morton. The day after, Diana and Mary quitted it for distant B—. In a week, Mr. Rivers and Hannah repaired to the parsonage : and so the old grange was abandoned.

CHAPTER V.

My home, then—when I at last find a home,—is a cottage: a little room with white-washed walls, and a sanded floor; containing four painted chairs and a table, a clock, a cupboard, with two or three plates and dishes, and a set of tea-things in delf. Above, a chamber of the same dimensions as the kitchen, with a deal bedstead, and chest of drawers; small, yet too large to be filled with my scanty wardrobe: though the kindness of my gentle and generous friends has increased that, by a modest stock of such things as are necessary.

It is evening. I have dismissed, with the fee of an orange, the little orphan who serves me as a handmaid. I am sitting alone on the hearth. This morning, the village school opened. I had twenty scholars. But three of the number can read: none write or cypher. Several knit, and a few sew a little. They speak with the broadest accent of the district. At present, they and I have a difficulty in understanding each other's language. Some of them are unmannered, rough, intractable, as well as ignorant; but others are docile, have a wish to learn, and evince a disposition that pleases me. I must not forget that these coarsely-clad little peasants are of flesh and blood as good as the scions of gentlest genealogy; and that the germs of native excellence, refinement, intelligence, kind feeling, are as likely to exist in their hearts as in those of the best-born. My duty will be to develope these germs: surely I shall find some happiness in discharging that office. Much enjoyment I do not expect in the life opening before me: yet it will, doubtless, if I regulate my mind, and exert my powers as I ought, yield me enough to live on from day to day.

Was I very gleeful, settled, content, during the hours I passed in yonder bare, humble schoolroom this morning and afternoon? Not to deceive myself, I must reply—No: I felt desolate to a degree. I felt—yes, idiot that I am—I felt degraded. I doubted I had taken a step which sank instead of raising me in the scale of social existence. I was weakly dismayed at the ignorance, the poverty, the coarseness of all I heard and saw round me. But let me not hate and despise my-

self too much for these feelings : I know them to
be wrong—that is a great step gained ; I shall
strive to overcome them. To-morrow, I trust, I
shall get the better of them partially ; and in a few
weeks, perhaps, they will be quite subdued. In a
few months, it is possible, the happiness of seeing
progress, and a change for the better in my scholars,
may substitute gratification for disgust.

Meantime, let me ask myself one question—
Which is better ?—To have surrendered to temptation ; listened to passion ; made no painful effort
—no struggle ;—but to have sunk down in the
silken snare ; fallen asleep on the flowers covering
it ; wakened in a southern clime, amongst the
luxuries of a pleasure-villa : to have been now living
in France, Mr. Rochester's mistress ; delirious with
his love half my time—for he would—oh, yes, he
would have loved me well for a while. He *did* love
me—no one will ever love me so again. I shall
never more know the sweet homage given to
beauty, youth, and grace—for never to any else
shall I seem to possess these charms. He was
fond and proud of me—it is what no man besides
will ever be.—But where am I wandering, and
what am I saying : and, above all, feeling ? Whether is it better, I ask, to be a slave in a fool's
paradise at Marseilles—fevered with delusive bliss
one hour—suffocating with the bitterest tears of

remorse and shame the next—or to be a village-schoolmistress, free and honest, in a breezy mountain nook in the healthy heart of England?

Yes; I feel now that I was right when I adhered to principle and law, and scorned and crushed the insane promptings of a frenzied moment. God directed me to a correct choice : I thank His providence for the guidance!

Having brought my eventide musings to this point, I rose, went to my door, and looked at the sunset of the harvest-day, and at the quiet fields before my cottage; which, with the school, was distant half a mile from the village. The birds were singing their last strains—

"The air was mild; the dew was balm."

While I looked, I thought myself happy, and was surprised to find myself erelong weeping—and why? For the doom which had reft me from adhesion to my master: for him I was no more to see; for the desperate grief and fatal fury—consequences of my departure—which might now, perhaps, be dragging him from the path of right, too far to leave hope of ultimate restoration thither. At this thought, I turned my face aside from the lovely sky of eve and lonely vale of Morton—I say lonely, for in that bend of it visible to me, there was no building apparent save the church and the parsonage, half-hid in trees; and, quite at the extremity, the roof of Vale-Hall, where the rich Mr. Oliver and his daughter lived. I hid my eyes, and leant my head against the stone frame of my door : but soon a slight noise near the wicket which shut in my tiny garden from the meadow beyond it, made me look up. A dog—old Carlo, Mr. Rivers' pointer, as I saw in a moment—was pushing the gate with his nose, and St. John himself leant upon it with folded arms; his brow knit, his gaze, grave almost to displeasure, fixed on me. I asked him to come in.

"No, I cannot stay : I have only brought you a little parcel my sisters left for you. I think it contains a colour-box, pencils, and paper."

I approached to take it : a welcome gift it was. He examined my face, I thought, with austerity, as I came near : the traces of tears were doubtless very visible upon it.

"Have you found your first day's work harder than you expected?" he asked.

"Oh, no! On the contrary, I think in time I shall get on with my scholars very well."

"But perhaps your accommodations—your cottage—your furniture—have disappointed your expectations? They are, in truth, scanty enough but"——I interrupted :

"My cottage is clean and weather-proof; my furniture sufficient and commodious. All I see has made me thankful, not despondent. I am not absolutely such a fool and sensualist as to regret the absence of a carpet, a sofa, and silver plate : besides, five weeks ago I had nothing—I was an outcast, a beggar, a vagrant ; now I have acquaintance, a home, a business. I wonder at the goodness of God ; the generosity of my friends ; the bounty of my lot. I do not repine."

"But you feel solitude an oppression ? The little house there behind you is dark and empty ?"

"I have hardly had time yet to enjoy a sense of tranquillity, much less to grow impatient under one of loneliness."

"Very well ; I hope you feel the content you express : at any rate, your good sense will tell you that it is too soon yet to yield to the vacillating fears of Lot's wife. What you had left before I saw you, of course I do not know ; but I counsel you to resist, firmly, every temptation which would incline you to look back : pursue your present career steadily, for some months at least."

"It is what I mean to do," I answered. St. John continued :—

"It is hard work to control the workings of inclination, and turn the bent of nature : but that it may be done, I know from experience. God has given us, in a measure, the power to make our own fate ; and when our energies seem to

demand a sustenance they cannot get—when our
will strains after a path we may not follow—we
need neither starve from inanition, nor stand still
in despair: we have but to seek another nourish-
ment for the mind, as strong as the forbidden
food it longed to taste—and perhaps purer; and to
hew out for the adventurous foot a road as direct
and broad as the one Fortune has blocked up
against us, if rougher than it.

"A year ago, I was myself intensely miserable,
because I thought I had made a mistake in entering the ministry: its uniform duties wearied me
to death. I burnt for the more active life of the
world—for the more exciting toils of a literary
career—for the destiny of an artist, author, orator;
anything, rather than that of a priest: yes, the
heart of a politician, of a soldier, of a votary of
glory, a lover of renown, a luster after power,
beat under my curate's surplice. I considered
my life was so wretched, it must be changed, or I
must die. After a season of darkness and struggling, light broke and relief fell: my cramped
existence all at once spread out to a plain without
bounds—my powers heard a call from heaven to
rise, gather their full strength, spread their wings
and mount beyond ken. God had an errand for
me; to bear which afar, to deliver it well, skill
and strength, courage and eloquence, the best

qualifications of soldier, statesman and orator, were all needed : for these all centre in the good missionary.

" A missionary I resolved to be. From that moment my state of mind changed : the fetters dissolved and dropped from every faculty, leaving nothing of bondage but its galling soreness—which time only can heal. My father, indeed, opposed the determination; but since his death, I have not a legitimate obstacle to contend with : some affairs settled, a successor for Morton provided, an entanglement or two of the feelings broken through or cut asunder—a last conflict with human weakness, in which I know I shall overcome, because I have vowed that I *will* overcome—and I leave Europe for the East."

He said this in his peculiar, subdued yet emphatic voice ; looking, when he had ceased speaking, not at me, but at the setting sun : at which I looked too. Both he and I had our backs towards the path leading up the field to the wicket. We had heard no step on that grass-grown track ; the water running in the vale was the one lulling sound of the hour and scene : we might well then start, when a gay voice, sweet as a silver bell, exclaimed :—

" Good evening, Mr. Rivers. And good evening, old Carlo. Your dog is quicker to recognize his friends than you are, sir : he pricked his ears and wagged his tail when I was at the bottom of the field, and you have your back towards me now."

It was true. Though Mr. Rivers had started at the first of those musical accents, as if a thunderbolt had split a cloud over his head, he stood yet, at the close of the sentence, in the same attitude in which the speaker had surprised him: his arm resting on the gate, his face directed towards the west. He turned at last, with measured deliberation. A vision, as it seemed to me, had risen at his side. There appeared, within three feet of him, a form clad in pure white—a youthful, graceful form: full, yet fine in contour; and when, after bending to caress Carlo, it lifted up its head, and threw back a long veil, there bloomed under his glance a face of perfect beauty. Perfect beauty is a strong expression; but I do not retrace or qualify it: as sweet features as ever the temperate clime of Albion moulded; as pure hues of rose and lily as ever her humid gales and vapoury skies generated and screened, justified, in this instance, the term. No charm was wanting, no defect was perceptible: the young girl had regular and delicate lineaments; eyes shaped and coloured as we see them in lovely pictures, large, and dark, and full; the

long and shadowy eyelash which encircles a fine
eye with so soft a fascination; the pencilled brow
which gives such clearness; the white, smooth
forehead, which adds such repose to the livelier
beauties of tint and ray; the cheek, oval, fresh
and smooth; the lips fresh too, ruddy, healthy,
sweetly formed; the even and gleaming teeth
without flaw; the small, dimpled chin; the ornament of rich, plenteous tresses,—all advantages, in
short, which combined, realize the ideal of beauty,
were fully hers. I wondered, as I looked at this
fair creature: I admired her with my whole heart.
Nature had surely formed her in a partial mood;
and forgetting her usual stinted step-mother dole
of gifts, had endowed this, her darling, with a
granddame's bounty.

What did St. John Rivers think of this earthly
angel? I naturally asked myself that question as
I saw him turn to her and look at' her; and, as
naturally, I sought the answer to the inquiry in
his countenance. He had already withdrawn his
eye from the Peri, and was looking at a humble
tuft of daisies which grew by the wicket.

"A lovely evening; but late for you to be out
alone," he said, as he crushed the snowy heads of
the closed flowers with his foot.

" Oh, I only came home from S—— (she mentioned the name of a large town some twenty

miles distant) this afternoon.   Papa told me you had opened your school, and that the new mistress was come; and so I put on my bonnet after tea and ran up the valley to see her: this is she?" pointing to me.

"It is," said St. John.

"Do you think you shall like Morton?" she asked of me; with a direct and naïve simplicity of tone and manner, pleasing, if child-like.

"I hope I shall. I have many inducements to do so."

" Did you find your scholars as attentive as you expected?"

" Quite."

" Do you like your house?"

" Very much."

" Have I furnished it nicely?"

" Very nicely indeed."

" And made a good choice of an attendant for you in Alice Wood?"

" You have indeed. She is teachable and handy." (This, then, I thought, is Miss Oliver, the heiress: favoured, it seems, in the gifts fo fortune, as well as in those of nature!   What happy combination of the planets presided over her birth, I wonder?)

" I shall come up and help you to teach sometimes" she added.   " It will be a change for me to visit you now and then: and I like a change. Mr. Rivers, I have been *so* gay during my stay at S—. Last night, or rather this morning, I was dancing till two o'clock. The ——th regiment are stationed there, since the riots; and the officers are the most agreeable men in the world: they put all our young knife-grinders and scissar merchants to shame."

It seemed to me that Mr. St. John's under lip protruded, and his upper lip curled a moment. His mouth certainly looked a good deal compressed, and the lower part of his face unusually stern and square, as the laughing girl gave him this information. He lifted his gaze, too, from the daisies, and turned it on her. An unsmiling, a searching, a meaning gaze it was. She answered it with a second laugh: and laughter well became her youth, her roses, her dimples, her bright eyes.

As he stood, mute and grave, she again fell to caressing Carlo. "Poor Carlo loves me," said she. "*He* is not stern and distant to his friends; and if he could speak, he would not be silent."

As she patted the dog's head, bending with native grace before his young and austere master, I saw a glow rise to that master's face.

I saw his solemn eye melt with sudden fire, and flicker with resistless emotion. Flushed and kindled thus, he looked nearly as beautiful for a man as she for a woman. His chest heaved once, as if his large heart, weary of despotic constriction, had expanded, despite the will, and made a vigorous bound for the attainment of liberty. But he curbed it, I think, as a resolute rider would curb a rearing steed. He responded neither by word nor movement to the gentle advances made him.

"Papa says you never come to see us now," continued Miss Oliver, looking up. "You are quite a stranger at Vale Hall. He is alone this evening, and not very well: will you return with me and visit him?"

"It is not a seasonable hour to intrude on Mr. Oliver," answered St. John.

"Not a seasonable hour! But, I declare, it is. It is just the hour when papa most wants company: when the works are closed, and he has no business to occupy him. Now, Mr. Rivers, *do* come. Why are you so very shy, and so very sombre?" She filled up the hiatus his silence left by a reply of her own.

"I forgot," she exclaimed, shaking her beautiful curled head, as if shocked at herself.

"I am so giddy and thoughtless! *Do* excuse me. It had slipped my memory that you have good reasons to be indisposed for joining in my chatter. Diana and Mary have left you, and Moor House is shut up, and you are so lonely. I am sure I pity you. Do come and see papa."

"Not to-night, Miss Rosamond, not to-night."

Mr. St. John spoke almost like an automaton: himself only knew the effort it cost him thus to refuse.

"Well, if you are so obstinate, I will leave you; for I dare not stay any longer: the dew begins to fall. Good-evening!"

She held out her hand. He just touched it. "Good-evening!" he repeated, in a voice low and hollow as an echo. She turned; but in a moment returned.

"Are you well?" she asked. Well might she put the question: his face was blanched as her gown.

"Quite well," he enunciated; and, with a bow, he left the gate. She went one way; he another. She turned twice to gaze after him, as she tripped fairy-like down the field; he, as he strode firmly across, never turned at all.

This spectacle of another's suffering and sacrifices, rapt my thoughts from exclusive meditation on my own. Diana Rivers had designated her brother "inexorable as death." She had not exaggerated.

CHAPTER VI.

I CONTINUED the labours of the village school as actively and faithfully as I could. It was truly hard work at first. Some time elapsed before, with all my efforts, I could comprehend my scholars and their nature. Wholly un-taught, with faculties quite torpid, they seemed to me hopelessly dull; and, at first sight, all dull alike: but I soon found I was mistaken. There was a difference amongst them as amongst the educated; and when I got to know them, and they me, this difference rapidly developed itself. Their amazement at me, my language, my rules and ways, once subsided, I found some of these heavy-looking, gaping rustics wake up into sharp-witted girls enough. Many showed themselves obliging, and amiable too; and I discovered amongst them not a few examples of natural politeness, and innate self-respect, as well as of excellent capacity, that

won both my good will and my admiration.
These soon took a pleasure in doing their work
well; in keeping their persons neat; in learning their tasks regularly; in acquiring quiet
and orderly manners. The rapidity of their
progress, in some instances, was even surpris-
ing; and an honest and happy pride I took in
it: besides, I began personally to like some of
the best girls; and they liked me. I had
amongst my scholars several farmers' daughters:
young women grown, almost. These could
already read, write, and sew; and to them I
taught the elements of grammar, geography,
history, and the finer kinds of needlework. I
found estimable characters amongst them—characters desirous of information, and disposed
for improvement—with whom I passed many a
pleasant evening hour in their own homes.
Their parents then (the farmer and his wife)
loaded me with attentions. There was an
enjoyment in accepting their simple kindness,
and in repaying it by a consideration—a scru-
pulous regard to their feelings—to which they
were not, perhaps, at all times accustomed,
and which both charmed and benefited them;
because, while it elevated them in their own
eyes, it made them emulous to merit the defe-
rential treatment they received.

I felt I became a favourite in the neighbourhood. Whenever I went out, I heard on all
sides cordial salutations, and was welcomed
with friendly smiles. To live amidst general
regard, though it be but the regard of working-
people, is like "sitting in sunshine, calm and
sweet:" serene inward feelings bud and bloom
under the ray. At this period of my life, my
heart far oftener swelled with thankfulness than
sunk with dejection: and yet, reader, to tell
you all, in the midst of this calm, this useful
existence—after a day passed in honourable
exertion amongst my scholars, an evening spent
in drawing or reading contentedly alone—I
used to rush into strange dreams at night:
dreams many coloured, agitated, full of the
ideal, the stirring, the stormy—dreams where,
amidst unusual scenes, charged with adventure,
with agitating risk and romantic chance, I still
again and again met Mr. Rochester, always at
some exciting crisis; and then the sense of
being in his arms, hearing his voice, meeting
his eye, touching his hand and cheek, loving
him, being loved by him—the hope of passing
a lifetime at his side, would be renewed, with
all its first force and fire. Then I awoke.
Then I recalled where I was, and how situated.
Then I rose up on my curtainless bed, trem-

bling and quivering; and then the still, dark
night witnessed the convulsion of despair, and
heard the burst of passion.   By nine o'clock
the next morning, I was punctually opening the
school; tranquil, settled, prepared for the steady
duties of the day.

Rosamond Oliver kept her word in coming
to visit me.   Her call at the school was generally made in the course of her morning ride.
She would canter up to the door on her pony,
followed by a mounted livery servant.   Anything more exquisite than her appearance, in
her purple habit, with her Amazon's cap of
black velvet placed gracefully above the long
curls that kissed her cheek and floated to her
shoulders, can scarcely be imagined : and it was
thus she would enter the rustic building, and
glide through the dazzled ranks of the village
children.   She generally came at the hour
when Mr. Rivers was engaged in giving his
daily catechising lesson.   Keenly, I fear, did
the eye of the visitress pierce the young pastor's heart.   A sort of instinct seemed to warn
him of her entrance, even when he did not see
it; and when he was looking quite away from
the door, if she appeared at it, his cheek would
glow, and his marble-seeming features, though
they refused to relax, changed indescribably;

and in their very quiescence became expressive of a repressed fervour, stronger than working muscle or darting glance could indicate.

Of course, she knew her power: indeed, he did not, because he could not, conceal it from her. In spite of his Christian stoicism, when she went up and addressed him, and smiled gaily, encouragingly, even fondly in his face, his hand would tremble, and his eye burn. He seemed to say, with his sad and resolute look, if he did not say it with his lips, "I love you, and I know you prefer me. It is not despair of success that keeps me dumb. If I offered my heart, I believe you would accept it. But that heart is already laid on a sacred altar: the fire is arranged round it. It will soon be no more than a sacrifice consumed."

And then she would pout like a disappointed child; a pensive cloud would soften her radiant vivacity; she would withdraw her hand hastily from his, and turn in transient petulance from his aspect, at once so heroic and so martyr-like. St. John, no doubt, would have given the world to follow, recall, retain her, when she thus left him: but he would not give one chance of Heaven; nor relinquish, for the ely-

sium of her love, one hope of the true, eternal
Paradise. Besides, he could not bound all that
he had in his nature—the rover, the aspirant,
the poet, the priest—in the limits of a single
passion. He could not—he would not—renounce his wild field of mission warfare for the
parlours and the peace of Vale Hall. I learnt
so much from himself, in an inroad I once,
despite his reserve, had the daring to make on
his confidence.

Miss Oliver already honoured me with frequent visits to my cottage. I had learnt her
whole character; which was without mystery or
disguise : she was coquettish, but not heartless;
exacting, but not worthlessly selfish. She had
been indulged from her birth, but was not
absolutely spoilt. She was hasty, but good-
humoured; vain (she could not help it, when
every glance in the glass showed her such a
flush of loveliness), but not affected; liberal-
handed; innocent of the pride of wealth; in-
genuous; sufficiently intelligent; gay, lively,
and unthinking: she was very charming, in
short, even to a cool observer of her own sex
like me ; but she was not profoundly interest-
ing or thoroughly impressive. A very different
sort of mind was hers from that, for instance, of
the sisters of St. John. Still, I liked her almost

as I liked my pupil Adèle: except that, for a child whom we have watched over and taught, a closer affection is engendered than we can give an equally attractive adult acquaintance.

She had taken an amiable caprice to me. She said I was like Mr. Rivers (only, certainly, she allowed, "not one-tenth so handsome; though I was a nice, neat little soul enough: but he was an angel"). I was, however, good, clever, composed, and firm, like him. I was a *lusus naturæ*, she affirmed, as a village-school-mistress: she was sure my previous history, if known, would make a delightful romance.

One evening, while with her usual child-like activity, and thoughtless yet not offensive inquisitiveness, she was rummaging the cupboard and the table-drawer of my little kitchen, she discovered first two French books, a volume of Schiller, a German grammar and dictionary; and then my drawing-materials and some sketches, including a pencil-head of a pretty little cherub-like girl, one of my scholars, and sundry views from nature, taken in the Vale of Morton and on the surrounding moors. She was first transfixed with surprise, and then electrified with delight.

"Had I done these pictures? Did I know French and German? What a love—what a miracle I was! I drew better than her master in the first school in S——. Would I sketch a portrait of her to show to papa?"

" With pleasure," I replied; and I felt a thrill of artist-delight at the idea of copying from so perfect and radiant a model. She had then on a dark-blue silk dress; her arms and her neck were bare; her only ornament was her chestnut tresses, which waved over her shoulders with all the wild grace of natural curls. I took a sheet of fine card-board, and drew a careful outline. I promised myself the pleasure of colouring it; and, as it was getting late then, I told her she must come and sit another day.

She made such a report of me to her father, that Mr. Oliver himself accompanied her next evening—a tall, massive-featured, middle-aged, and grey-headed man, at whose side his lovely daughter looked like a bright flower near a hoary turret. He appeared a taciturn, and per-haps a proud personage; but he was very kind to me. The sketch of Rosamond's portrait pleased him highly: he said I must make a finished picture of it. He insisted, too, on my coming the next day to spend the evening at Vale-Hall.

I went. I found it a large, handsome resi-dence, shewing abundant evidences of wealth in the proprietor. Rosamond was full of glee and pleasure all the time I stayed. Her father was affable; and when he entered into conversation with me after tea, he expressed in strong terms his approbation of what I had done in Morton school; and said he only feared, from what he saw and heard, I was too good for the place, and would soon quit it for one more suitable.

"Indeed!" cried Rosamond, "she is clever enough to be a governess in a high family, papa."

I thought—I would far rather be where I am than in any high family in the land. Mr. Oliver spoke of Mr. Rivers—of the Rivers' family—with great respect. He said it was a very old name in that neighbourhood; that the ancestors of the house were wealthy; that all Morton had once belonged to them; that even now he considered the representative of that house might, if he liked, make an alliance with the best. He accounted it a pity that so fine and talented a young man should have formed the design of going out as a missionary: it was quite throwing a valuable life away. It appeared, then, that her father would throw no obstacle in the way of Rosamond's union with St. John. Mr. Oliver evidently regarded the young clergyman's good birth, old name, and sacred profession, as sufficient compensation for the want of fortune.

It was the fifth of November, and a holiday. My little servant, after helping me to clean my house, was gone; well satisfied with the fee of a penny for her aid. All about me was spotless and bright—scoured floor, polished grate, and well-rubbed chairs. I had also made myself neat, and had now the afternoon before me to spend as I would.

The translation of a few pages of German occupied an hour; then I got my palette and pencils, and fell to the more soothing, because easier occupation, of completing Rosamond Oliver's miniature. The head was finished already : there was but the background to tint, and the drapery to shade off; a touch of carmine, too, to add to the ripe lips—a soft curl here and there to the tresses—a deeper tinge to the shadow of the lash under the azured eyelid. I was absorbed in the execution of these nice details, when, after one rapid tap, my door unclosed, admitting St. John Rivers.

"I am come to see how you are spending your holiday," he said. "Not, I hope, in thought? No, that is well : while you draw you will not feel lonely. You see, I mistrust you still : though you have borne up wonderfully so far. I have brought you a book for evening solace," and he laid on the table a new publication—a poem: one of those genuine productions so often vouchsafed to the fortunate public of those days—the golden age of modern literature. Alas! the readers of our era are less favoured. But, courage! I will not pause either to accuse or repine. I know poetry is not dead, nor genius lost; nor has Mammon gained power over either, to bind or slay: they will both assert their existence, their presence, their liberty, and strength again one day. Powerful angels, safe in heaven! they smile when sordid souls triumph, and feeble ones weep over their destruction. Poetry destroyed? Genius banished? No! Mediocrity, no: do not let envy prompt you to the thought. No; they not only live, but reign, and redeem: and without their divine influence spread everywhere, you would be in hell—the hell of your own meanness.

While I was eagerly glancing at the bright pages of Marmion (for Marmion it was), St. John stooped to examine my drawing. His tall figure sprang erect again with a start: he said nothing. I looked up at him: he shunned my eye. I knew his thoughts well, and could read his heart plainly; at the moment I felt

calmer and cooler than he : I had then tem-
porarily the advantage of him ; and I conceived
an inclination to do him some good, if I could.

"With all his firmness and self-control,"
thought I, "he tasks himself too far : locks
every feeling and pang within—expresses, con-
fesses, imparts nothing. I am sure it would
benefit him to talk a little about this sweet
Rosamond, whom he thinks he ought not to
marry : I will make him talk."

I said first : "Take a chair, Mr. Rivers."
But he answered, as he always did, that he
could not stay. "Very well," I responded,
mentally, "stand, if you like ; but you shall
not go just yet, I am determined : solitude is
at least as bad for you as it is for me. I'll try
if I cannot discover the secret spring of your
confidence, and find an aperture in that
marble breast through which I can shed one
drop of the balm of sympathy."

"Is this portrait like?" I asked, bluntly.

"Like! Like whom? I did not observe it
closely."

"You did, Mr. Rivers."

He almost started at my sudden and strange
abruptness : he looked at me astonished. *
"Oh, that is nothing yet," I muttered within.
I don't mean to be baffled by a little stiffness

on your part : I'm prepared to go to considerable lengths." I continued, "You observed it closely and distinctly : but I have no objection to your looking at it again," and I rose and placed it in his hand.

"A well-executed picture," he said; "very soft, clear colouring ; very graceful and correct drawing."

"Yes, yes; I know all that. But what of the resemblance? Who is it like?"

Mastering some hesitation, he answered, "Miss Oliver, I presume."

"Of course. And now, sir, to reward you for the accurate guess, I will promise to paint you a careful and faithful duplicate of this very picture, provided you admit that the gift would be acceptable to you. I don't wish to throw away my time and trouble on an offering you would deem worthless."

He continued to gaze at the picture : the longer he looked, the firmer he held it, the more he seemed to covet it. "It is like!" he murmured; "the eye is well managed : the colour, light, expression, are perfect. It smiles!"

"Would it comfort, or would it wound you to have a similar painting? Tell me that. When you are at Madagascar, or at the Cape, or in India, would it be a consolation to have that memento in your possession; or would the sight of it bring recollections calculated to enervate and distress?"

He now furtively raised his eyes: he glanced at me irresolute, disturbed: he again surveyed the picture.

"That I should like to have it is certain: whether it would be judicious or wise is another question."

Since I had ascertained that Rosamond really preferred him, and that her father was not likely to oppose the match, I—less exalted in my views than St. John—had been strongly disposed in my own heart to advocate their union. It seemed to me that, should he become the possessor of Mr. Oliver's large fortune, he might do as much good with it as if he went and laid his genius out to wither, and his strength to waste, under a tropical sun. With this persuasion, I now answered:—

" As far as I can see, it would be wiser and more judicious if you were to take to yourself the original at once."

By this time he had sat down: he had laid the picture on the table before him, and, with his brow supported on both hands, hung fondly over it. I discerned he was now neither angry nor shocked at my audacity. I saw even that

to be thus frankly addressed on a subject he
had deemed unapproachable—to hear it thus
freely handled—was beginning to be felt by
him as a new pleasure—an unhoped-for relief.
Reserved people often really need the frank
discussion of their sentiments and griefs more
than the expansive. The sternest-seeming
stoic is human after all; and to " burst" with
boldness and good will into " the silent sea" of
their souls, is often to confer on them the first of
obligations.

" She likes you, I am sure," said I, as I stood
behind his chair, " and her father respects you.
Moreover, she is a sweet girl—rather thoughtless; but you would have sufficient thought for
both yourself and her. You ought to marry
her."

" *Does* she like me?" he asked.

" Certainly; better than she likes any one
else. She talks of you continually : there is no
subject she enjoys so much, or touches upon so
often."

" It is very pleasant to hear this," he said—
" very : go on for another quarter of an hour."
And he actually took out his watch and laid it
upon the table to measure the time.

" But where is the use of going on," I asked,
" when you are probably preparing some iron

blow of contradiction, or forging a fresh chain to fetter your heart?"

"Don't imagine such hard things. Fancy me yielding and melting, as I am doing: human love rising like a freshly opened fountain in my mind, and overflowing with sweet inundation all the field I have so carefully, and with such labour, prepared—so assiduously sown with the seeds of good intentions, of self-denying plans. And now it is deluged with a nectarous flood —the young germs swamped—delicious poison cankering them: now I see myself stretched on an ottoman in the drawing-room at Vale Hall, at my bride Rosamond Oliver's feet: she is talking to me with her sweet voice—gazing down on me with those eyes your skilful hand has copied so well—smiling at me with these coral lips. She is mine—I am hers—this present life and passing world suffice to me. Hush! say nothing—my heart is full of delight—my senses are entranced—let the time I marked pass in peace."

I humoured him: the watch ticked on: he breathed fast and low: I stood silent. Amidst this hush the quarter sped: he replaced the watch, laid the picture down, rose, and stood on the hearth.

"Now," said he, "that little space was given

to delirium and delusion. I rested my temples on the breast of temptation, and put my neck voluntarily under her yoke of flowers; I tasted her cup. The pillow was burning: there is an asp in the garland: the wine has a bitter taste: her promises are hollow—her offers false: I see and know all this."

I gazed at him in wonder.

"It is strange," pursued he, "that while I love Rosamond Oliver so wildly—with all the intensity, indeed, of a first passion, the object of which is exquisitely beautiful, graceful, and fascinating—I experience at the same time a calm, unwarped consciousness, that she would not make me a good wife; that she is not the partner suited to me; that I should discover this within a year after marriage; and that to twelve months' rapture would succeed a lifetime of regret. This I know."

"Strange, indeed!" I could not help ejaculating.

"While something in me," he went on, "is acutely sensible to her charms, something else is as deeply impressed with her defects: they are such that she could sympathize in nothing I aspired to—co-operate in nothing I undertook. Rosamond a sufferer, a labourer, a female apostle? Rosamond a missionary's wife? No!"

"But you need not be a missionary. You might relinquish that scheme."

"Relinquish! What—my vocation? My great work? My foundation laid on earth for a mansion in heaven? My hopes of being numbered in the band who have merged all ambitions in the glorious one of bettering their race—of carrying knowledge into the realms of ignorance—of substituting peace for war—freedom for bondage—religion for superstition—the hope of heaven for the fear of hell? Must I relinquish that? It is dearer than the blood in my veins. It is what I have to look forward to, and to live for."

After a considerable pause, I said—"And Miss Oliver? Are her disappointment and sorrow of no interest to you?"

"Miss Oliver is ever surrounded by suitors and flatterers: in less than a month, my image will be effaced from her heart. She will forget me; and will marry, probably, some one who will make her far happier than I should do."

"You speak coolly enough; but you suffer in the conflict. You are wasting away."

"No. If I get a little thin, it is with anxiety about my prospects, yet unsettled—my departure, continually procrastinated. Only this morning, I received intelligence that the

successor, whose arrival I have been so long
expecting, cannot be ready to replace me for
three months to come yet: and perhaps the
three months may extend to six."

" You tremble and become flushed whenever
Miss Oliver enters the schoolroom."

Again the surprised expression crossed his
face. He had not imagined that a woman
would dare to speak so to a man. For me, I
felt at home in this sort of discourse. I could
never rest in communication with strong, dis-
creet, and refined minds, whether male or female, till I had passed the outworks of con-
ventional reserve, and crossed the threshold of
confidence, and won a place by their heart's
very hearthstone.

" You *are* original," said he, " and not timid.
There is something brave in your spirit, as well as
penetrating in your eye : but allow me to assure
you that you partially misinterpret my emotions.
You think them more profound and potent than
they are. You give me a larger allowance of
sympathy than I have a just claim to. When
I colour, and when I shake before Miss Oliver,
I do not pity myself. I scorn the weakness.
I know it is ignoble ; a mere fever of the flesh :
not, I declare, a convulsion of the soul. *That*
is just as fixed as a rock, firm set in the depths

of a restless sea.   Know me to be what I am—
a cold, hard man."

I smiled incredulously.

"You have taken my confidence by storm,"
he continued; "and now it is much at your
service.   I am simply, in my original state—
stripped of that blood-bleached robe with
which Christianity covers human deformity—a
cold, hard, ambitious man.   Natural affection
only, of all the sentiments, has permanent
power over me.   Reason, and not Feeling, is
my guide: my ambition is unlimited; my desire to rise higher, to do more than others,
insatiable.   I honour endurance, perseverance,
industry, talent; because these are the means
by which men achieve great ends, and mount
to lofty eminence.   I watch your career with
interest, because I consider you a specimen of
a diligent, orderly, energetic woman: not because I deeply compassionate what you have
gone through, or what you still suffer."

"You would describe yourself as a mere
pagan philosopher," I said.

"No.   There is this difference between me
and deistic philosophers: I believe; and I
believe the Gospel.   You missed your epithet.
I am not a pagan, but a Christian philosopher
—a follower of the sect of Jesus.   As his

disciple, I adopt his pure, his merciful, his benignant doctrines. I advocate them : I am sworn to spread them. Won in youth to religion, she has cultivated my original qualities thus :—From the minute germ, natural affection, she has developed the overshadowing tree, philanthropy. From the wild, stringy root of human uprightness, she has reared a due sense of the Divine justice. Of the ambition to win power and renown for my wretched self, she has formed the ambition to spread my Master's kingdom ; to achieve victories for the standard of the cross. So much has religion done for me; turning the original materials to the best account: pruning and training nature. But she could not eradicate nature : nor will it be eradicated "till this mortal shall put on immortality."

Having said this, he took his hat, which lay on the table beside my palette. Once more he looked at the portrait.

"She *is* lovely," he murmured. "She is well named the Rose of the World, indeed !"

"And may I not paint one like it for you ?"

"*Cui bono?* No."

He drew over the picture the sheet of thin paper on which I was accustomed to rest my hand in painting to prevent the card-board from being sullied. What he suddenly saw on this blank paper, it was impossible for me to tell: but something had caught his eye. He took it up with a snatch; he looked at the edge; then shot a glance at me, inexpressibly peculiar, and quite incomprehensible: a glance that seemed to take and make note of every point in my shape, face, and dress; for it traversed all, quick, keen as lightning. His lips parted, as if to speak: but he checked the coming sentence, whatever it was.

"What is the matter?" I asked.

"Nothing in the world," was the reply; and, replacing the paper, I saw him dexterously tear a narrow slip from the margin. It disappeared in his glove; and, with one hasty nod and "good-afternoon," he vanished.

"Well!" I exclaimed, using an expression of the district; "that caps the globe, however!"

I, in my turn, scrutinized the paper; but saw nothing on it, save a few dingy stains of paint, where I had tried the tint in my pencil. I pondered the mystery a minute or two; but finding it insolvable, and being certain it could not be of much moment, I dismissed, and soon forgot it.

CHAPTER VII.

WHEN Mr. St. John went, it was beginning to snow: the whirling storm continued all night. The next day a keen wind brought fresh and blinding falls: by twilight the valley was drifted up and almost impassable. I had closed my shutter, laid a mat to the door to prevent the snow from blowing in under it, trimmed my fire, and after sitting nearly an hour on the hearth listening to the muffled fury of the tempest, I lit a candle, took down Marmion and beginning—

> " Day set on Norham's castled steep,
> And Tweed's fair river broad and deep,
> And Cheviot mountains lone;
> The massive towers, the donjon keep,
> The flanking walls that round them sweep,
> In yellow lustre shone."

I soon forgot storm in music.

I heard a noise: the wind, I thought, shook the door. No; it was St. John Rivers, who, lifting the latch, came in out of the frozen hurricane—the howling darkness—and stood before me; the cloak that covered his tall figure all white as a glacier. I was almost in consternation; so little had I expected any guest from the blocked-up vale that night.

"Any ill news?" I demanded. "Has anything happened?"

"No. How very easily alarmed you are!" he answered, removing his cloak and hanging it up against the door: towards which he again coolly pushed the mat which his entrance had deranged. He stamped the snow from his boots.

"I shall sully the purity of your floor;" said he, "but you must excuse me for once." Then he approached the fire: "I have had hard work to get here, I assure you," he observed, as he warmed his hands over the flame. "One drift took me up to the waist: happily the snow is quite soft yet."

"But why are you come?" I could not forbear saying.

"Rather an inhospitable question to put to a visitor; but since you ask it, I answer, simply to have a little talk with you: I got tired of my mute books and empty rooms. Besides, since yesterday, I have experienced the excitement of a person to whom a tale has been half-told, and who is impatient to hear the sequel."

He sat down. I recalled his singular conduct of yesterday, and really I began to fear his wits were touched. If he were insane, however, his was a very cool and collected insanity: I had never seen that handsome-featured face of his, look more like chiselled marble than it did just now; as he put aside his snow-wet hair from his forehead and let the fire-light shine free on his pale brow and cheek as pale: where it grieved me to discover the hollow trace of care or sorrow now so plainly graved. I waited, expecting he would say something I could at least comprehend; but his hand was now at his chin, his finger on his lip: he was thinking. It struck me that his hand looked wasted like his face. A perhaps uncalled-for gush of pity came over my heart: I was moved to say :—

"I wish Diana or Mary would come and live with you: it is too bad that you should be quite alone; and you are recklessly rash about your own health."

"Not at all," said he: "I care for mysel when necessary: I am well now. What do you see amiss in me?"

This was said with a careless, abstracted indifference, which showed that my solicitude
was, at least in his opinion, wholly superfluous.
I was silenced.

He still slowly moved his finger over his
upper lip, and still his eye dwelt dreamily on
the glowing grate : thinking it urgent to say
something, I asked him presently if he felt
any cold draught from the door, which was
behind him.

"No, no ;" he responded shortly and somewhat testily.

"Well," I reflected; "if you won't talk,
you may be still: I'll let you alone now and
return to my book."

So I snuffed the candle, and resumed
the perusal of Marmion. He soon stirred ;
my eye was instantly drawn to his move-
ments : he only took out a morocco pocket-
book, thence produced a letter which he read
in silence, folded it, put it back, relapsed into
meditation. It was vain to try to read with
such an inscrutable fixture before me ; nor
could I, in my impatience, consent to be dumb:
he might rebuff me if he liked, but talk I
would.

"Have you heard from Diana and Mary
lately ?"

"Not since the letter I showed you a week ago."

"There has not been any change made about your own arrangements? You will not be summoned to leave England sooner than you expected?"

"I fear not, indeed: such chance is too good to befall me." Baffled so far, I changed my ground—I bethought myself to talk about the school and my scholars.

"Mary Garrett's mother is better, and Mary came back to the school this morning, and I shall have four new girls next week from the Foundry Close—they would have come to-day but for the snow."

"Indeed?"

"Mr. Oliver pays for two."

"Does he?"

"He means to give the whole school a treat at Christmas."

"I know."

"Was it your suggestion?".

"No."

"Whose then?"

"His daughter's, I think."

"It is like her: she is so good-natured."

"Yes."

Again came the blank of a pause: the clock

struck eight strokes. It aroused him; he un-
crossed his legs, sat erect, turned to me.

" Leave your book a moment, and come a
little nearer the fire," he said.

Wondering, and of my wonder finding no
end, I complied.

" Half an hour ago," he pursued, " I spoke
of my impatience to hear the sequel of a tale :
on reflection, I find the matter will be better
managed by my assuming the narrator's part,
and converting you into a listener. Before
commencing, it is but fair to warn you that the
story will sound somewhat hackneyed in your
ears : but stale details often regain a degree of
freshness when they pass through new lips.
For the rest, whether trite or novel, it is
short.

"Twenty years ago, a poor curate—never mind
his name at this moment—fell in love with a
rich man's daughter: she fell in love with him,
and married him, against the advice of all her
friends; who consequently disowned her immediately after the wedding. Before two years
passed, the rash pair were both dead, and laid
quietly side by side under one slab. (I have
seen their grave; it formed part of the pavement of a huge churchyard surrounding the
grim, soot-black old cathedral of an overgrown

manufacturing town in ——shire.) They left
a daughter, which, at its very birth, Charity
received in her lap—cold as that of the snow-
drift I almost stuck fast in to-night. Charity
carried the friendless thing to the house of its
rich, maternal relations; it was reared by an
aunt-in-law, called (I come to names now)
Mrs. Reed of Gateshead—you start—did you
hear a noise? I daresay it is only a rat
scrambling along the rafters of the adjoining
schoolroom: it was a barn before I had it repaired and altered, and barns are generally
haunted by rats. To proceed. Mrs. Reed
kept the orphan ten years: whether it was
happy or not with her, I cannot say, never
having been told; but at the end of that time
she transferred it to a place you know—being
no other than Lowood school, where you so
long resided yourself. It seems her career
there was very honourable: from a pupil, she
became a teacher, like yourself — really it
strikes me there are parallel points in her history and yours—she left it to be a governess:
there, again, your fates were analogous; she
undertook the education of the ward of a certain Mr. Rochester."

" Mr. Rivers!" I interrupted.

"I can guess your feelings," he said, "but

restrain them for a while: I have nearly finished; hear me to the end. Of Mr. Rochester's character I know nothing, but the one fact that he professed to offer honourable marriage to this young girl, and that at the very altar she discovered he had a wife yet alive, though a lunatic. What his subsequent conduct and proposals were is a matter of pure conjecture; but when an event transpired which rendered inquiry after the governess necessary, it was discovered she was gone—no one could tell when, where, or how. She had left Thornfield Hall in the night; every research after her course had been vain: the country had been scoured far and wide; no vestige of information could be gathered respecting her. Yet that she should be found is become a matter of serious urgency: advertisements have been put in all the papers; I myself have received a letter from one Mr. Briggs, a solicitor, communicating the details I have just imparted. Is it not an odd tale?"

"Just tell me this," said I, "and since you know so much, you surely *can* tell it me— what of Mr. Rochester? How and where is he? What is he doing? Is he well?"

"I am ignorant of all concerning Mr. Rochester: the letter never mentions him but to narrate the fraudulent and illegal attempt I have adverted to. You should rather ask the name of the governess—the nature of the event which requires her appearance."

"Did no one go to Thornfield Hall then? Did no one see Mr. Rochester?"

"I suppose not."

"But they wrote to him?"

"Of course."

"And what did he say? Who has his letters?"

"Mr. Briggs intimates that the answer to his application was not from Mr. Rochester but from a lady: it is signed 'Alice Fairfax.'"

I felt cold and dismayed; my worst fears then were probably true: he had in all probability left England and rushed in reckless desperation to some former haunt on the continent. And what opiate for his severe sufferings—what object for his strong passions—had he sought there? I dared not answer the question. Oh, my poor master—once almost my husband—whom I had often called " my dear Edward!"

"He must have been a bad man," observed Mr. Rivers.

"You don't know him—don't pronounce an opinion upon him," I said with warmth.

"Very well," he answered quietly; "and indeed my head is otherwise occupied than with him : I have my tale to finish. Since you won't ask the governess's name, I must tell it of my own accord—stay—I have it here—it is always more satisfactory to see important points written down, fairly committed to black and white."

And the pocket-book was again deliberately produced, opened, sought through; from one of its compartments was extracted a shabby. slip of paper, hastily torn off: I recognised in its texture and its stains of ultra-marine, and lake, and vermilion, the ravished margin of the portrait-cover. He got up, held it close to my eyes; and I read, traced in Indian ink, in my own handwriting, the words "JANE EYRE"—the work doubtless of some moment of abstraction.

"Briggs wrote to me of a Jane Eyre;" he said, "the advertisements demanded a Jane Eyre : I knew a Jane Elliot.—I confess I had my suspicions, but it was only yesterday afternoon they were at once resolved into certainty. You own the name and renounce the *alias?*"

"Yes—yes—but where is Mr. Briggs? He perhaps knows more of Mr. Rochester than you do."

" Briggs is in London; I should doubt his knowing anything at all about Mr. Rochester: it is not in Mr. Rochester he is interested. Meantime, you forget essential points in pursuing trifles: you do not inquire why Mr. Briggs sought after you—what he wanted with you."

"Well, what did he want?"

" Merely to tell you that your uncle, Mr. Eyre of Madeira, is dead; that he has left you all his property, and that you are now rich— merely that—nothing more."

" I! rich?"

" Yes, you, rich—quite an heiress."

Silence succeeded.

" You must prove your identity of course," resumed St. John presently: " a step which will offer no difficulties; you can then enter on immediate possession. Your fortune is vested in the English funds: Briggs has the will and the necessary documents."

Here was a new card turned up! It is a fine thing, reader, to be lifted in a moment from indigence to wealth—a very fine thing: but not a matter one can comprehend, or consequently enjoy, all at once. And then there are other chances in life far more thrilling and rapture-giving: *this* is solid, an affair of the actual world, nothing ideal about it: all its associations are solid and sober, and its manifestations are the same. One does not jump, and spring, and shout hurrah! at hearing one has got a fortune; one begins to consider responsibilities, and to ponder business: on a base of steady satisfaction rise certain grave cares—and we contain ourselves, and brood over our bliss with a solemn brow.

Besides, the words Legacy, Bequest, go side by side with the words Death, Funeral. My uncle I had heard was dead—my only relative; ever since being made aware of his existence, I had cherished the hope of one day seeing him: now, I never should. And then this money came only to me: not to me and a re-joicing family, but to my isolated self. It was a grand boon doubtless; and independence would be glorious—yes, I felt that—*that* thought swelled my heart."

" You unbend your forehead at last," said Mr. Rivers: " I thought Medusa had looked at you, and that you were turning to stone—perhaps now you will ask how much you are worth?"

" How much am I worth?"

" Oh, a trifle! Nothing of course to speak of—twenty thousand pounds, I think they say—but what is that?"

"Twenty thousand pounds!"

Here was a new stunner—I had been calculating on four or five thousand. This news actually took my breath for a moment: Mr. St. John, whom I had never heard laugh before, laughed now.

"Well," said he, "if you had committed a murder, and I had told you your crime was discovered, you could scarcely look more aghast."

"It is a large sum—don't you think there is a mistake?"

"No mistake at all."

"Perhaps you have read the figures wrong —it may be 2000?"

"It is written in letters, not figures,—twenty thousand."

I again felt rather like an individual of but average gastronomical powers, sitting down to feast alone at a table spread with provisions for a hundred. Mr. Rivers rose now and put his cloak on.

"If it were not such a very wild night," he said, "I would send Hannah down to keep you company: you look too desperately miserable to be left alone. But Hannah, poor woman! could not stride the drifts so well as

I; her legs are not quite so long: so I must e'en leave you to your sorrows. Good-night."

He was lifting the latch: a sudden thought occurred to me.

"Stop one minute!" I cried.

"Well?"

"It puzzles me to know why Mr. Briggs wrote to you about me; or how he knew you, or could fancy that you, living in such an out-of-the-way place, had the power to aid in my discovery."

"Oh! I am a clergyman," he said; "and the clergy are often appealed to about odd matters." Again the latch rattled.

"No: that does not satisfy me!" I exclaimed: and, indeed, there was something in the hasty and unexplanatory reply, which, instead of allaying, piqued my curiosity more than ever.

"It is a very strange piece of business," I added: "I must know more about it."

"Another time."

"No: to-night!—to-night!" and as he turned from the door, I placed myself between it and him. He looked rather embarrassed.

"You certainly shall not go till you have told me all!" I said.

"I would rather not, just now."

"You shall!—you must!"

"I would rather Diana or Mary informed you."

Of course these objections wrought my eagerness to a climax : gratified it must be, and that without delay ; and I told him so.

"But I apprised you that I was a hard man," said he ; "difficult to persuade."

"And I am a hard woman,—impossible to put off."

"And then," he pursued, "I am cold : no fervour infects me."

"Whereas I am hot, and fire dissolves ice. The blaze there has thawed all the snow from your cloak ; by the same token, it has streamed on to my floor, and made it like a trampled street. As you hope ever to be forgiven, Mr. Rivers, the high crime and misdemeanor of spoiling a sanded kitchen, tell me what I wish to know."

"Well, then," he said, "I yield ; if not to your earnestness, to your perseverance : as stone is worn by continual dropping. Besides, you must know some day,—as well now as later. Your name is Jane Eyre ?"

"Of course : that was all settled before."

"You are not, perhaps, aware that I am your namesake?—that I was christened St. John Eyre Rivers ?"

"No, indeed! I remember now seeing the letter E comprised in your initials written in books you have at different times lent me; but I never asked for what name it stood. But what then? Surely——"

I stopped: I could not trust myself to entertain, much less to express, the thought that rushed upon me—that embodied itself,—that, in a second, stood out a strong, solid probability. Circumstances knit themselves, fitted themselves, shot into order: the chain that had been lying hitherto a formless lump of links, was drawn out straight,—every ring was perfect, the connection complete. I knew, by instinct, how the matter stood, before St. John had said another word: but I cannot expect the reader to have the same intuitive perception, so I must repeat his explanation.

"My mother's name was Eyre: she had two brothers; one a clergyman, who married Miss Jane Reed, of Gateshead; the other, John Eyre, Esq., merchant, late of Funchal, Madeira. Mr. Briggs, being Mr. Eyre's solicitor, wrote to us last August to inform us of our uncle's death; and to say that he had left his property to his brother the clergyman's orphan daughter; overlooking us, in consequence of a quarrel, never forgiven, between him and my father. He wrote again a few weeks since, to intimate that the heiress was lost; and asking if we knew anything of her. A name casually written on a slip of paper has enabled me to find her out. You know the rest." Again he was going, but I set my back against the door.

" Do let me speak," I said; "let me have one moment to draw breath and reflect." I paused —he stood before me, hat in hand, looking composed enough. I resumed :—

" Your mother was my father's sister."

" Yes."

" My aunt, consequently ?"

He bowed.

" My uncle John was your uncle John ? You, Diana, and Mary, are his sister's children; as I am his brother's child ?"

" Undeniably."

" You three, then, are my cousins : half our blood on each side flows from the same source ?"

" We are cousins : yes."

I surveyed him. It seemed I had found a brother : one I could be proud of,—one I could love; and two sisters, whose qualities were such, that when I knew them but as mere strangers, they had inspired me with genuine affection and admiration. The two girls, on whom, kneeling down on the wet ground, and looking through the low, latticed window of Moor House kitchen, I had gazed with so bitter a mixture of interest and despair, were my near kinswomen; and the young and stately gentleman who had found me almost dying at his threshold, was my blood relation. Glorious discovery to a lonely wretch! This was wealth indeed!—wealth to the heart!—a mine of pure, genial affections. This was a blessing, bright, vivid, and exhilarating!—not like the ponderous gift of gold: rich and welcome enough in its way, but sobering from its weight. I now clapped my hands in sudden joy—my pulse bounded, my veins thrilled.

"Oh, I am glad!—I am glad!" I exclaimed.

St. John smiled. "Did I not say you neglected essential points to pursue trifles?" he asked. "You were serious when I told you you had got a fortune; and now, for a matter of no moment, you are excited."

"What *can* you mean? It may be of no moment to you: you have sisters, and don't care for a cousin; but I had nobody; and now three relations,—or two, if you don't choose to be counted,—are born into my world, full grown. I say again, I am glad!"

I walked fast through the room: I stopped, half suffocated with the thoughts that rose faster than I could receive, comprehend, settle them :—thoughts of what might, could, would, and should be, and that ere long. I looked at the blank wall : it seemed a sky, thick with ascending stars,—every one lit me to a purpose or delight. Those who had saved my life, whom, till this hour, I had loved barrenly, I could now benefit. They were under a yoke : I could free them; they were scattered,—I could reunite them—the independence, the affluence which was mine, might be theirs too. Were we not four? Twenty thousand pounds shared equally, would be five thousand each,—enough and to spare : justice would be done,—mutual happiness secured. Now the wealth did not weigh on me : now it was not a mere bequest of coin,—it was a legacy of life, hope, enjoyment.

How I looked while these ideas were taking my spirit by storm, I cannot tell; but I perceived soon that Mr. Rivers had placed a chair behind me, and was gently attempting to make me sit down on it. He also advised me to be composed. I scorned the insinuation of helplessness and distraction, shook off his hand, and began to walk about again.

"Write to Diana and Mary to-morrow," I said, "and tell them to come home directly: Diana said they would both consider themselves rich with a thousand pounds, so with five thousand, they will do very well."

"Tell me where I can get you a glass of water," said St. John; "you must really make an effort to tranquillize your feelings."

"Nonsense! and what sort of an effect will the bequest have on you? Will it keep you in England, induce you to marry Miss Oliver, and settle down like an ordinary mortal?"

"You wander: your head becomes confused. I have been too abrupt in communicating the news: it has excited you beyond your strength."

"Mr. Rivers! you quite put me out of patience; I am rational enough; it is you who misunderstand; or rather, who affect to misunderstand."

"Perhaps if you explained yourself a little more fully, I should comprehend better."

"Explain! What is there to explain? You cannot fail to see that twenty thousand pounds, the sum in question, divided equally between the nephew and three nieces of our uncle, will give five thousand to each? What I want is, that you should write to your sisters and tell them of the fortune that has accrued to them."

"To you, you mean."

"I have intimated my view of the case: I am incapable of taking any other. I am not brutally selfish, blindly unjust, or fiendishly ungrateful. Besides, I am resolved I will have a home and connections. I like Moor-House, and I will live at Moor-House; I like Diana, and Mary, and I will attach myself for life to Diana and Mary. It would please and benefit me to have five thousand pounds; it would torment and oppress me to have twenty thousand: which, moreover, could never be mine in justice, though it might in law. I abandon to you, then, what is absolutely super-fluous to me. Let there be no opposition, and no discussion about it: let us agree amongst each other, and decide the point at once."

"This is acting on first impulses: you must take days to consider such a matter, ere your word can be regarded as valid."

"Oh! if all you doubt is my sincerity, I am easy: you see the justice of the case?"

"I *do* see a certain justice; but it is contrary

to all custom. Besides the entire fortune is your
right : my uncle gained it by his own efforts ;
he was free to leave it to whom he would : he
left it to you. After all, justice permits you to
keep it : you may, with a clear conscience, consider it absolutely your own."

"With me," said I, "it is fully as much a
matter of feeling as of conscience : I must indulge my feelings ; I so seldom have had an
opportunity of doing so. Were you to argue,
object, and annoy me for a year, I could not
forego the delicious pleasure of which I have
caught a glimpse—that of repaying, in part, a
mighty obligation, and winning to myself life-
long friends."

"You think so now," rejoined St. John ;
"because you do not know what it is to possess, nor consequently to enjoy wealth : you
cannot form a notion of the importance twenty
thousand pounds would give you ; of the place
it would enable you to take in society ; of the
prospects it would open to you : you cannot ——"

"And you," I interrupted, "cannot at all
imagine the craving I have for fraternal and
sisterly love. I never had a home, I never had
brothers or sisters ; I must and will have them
now : you are not reluctant to admit me and
own me, are you ?"

"Jane: I will be your brother—my sisters will be your sisters—without stipulating for this sacrifice of your just rights."

"Brother? Yes; at the distance of a thousand leagues! Sisters? Yes; slaving amongst strangers! I, wealthy—gorged with gold I never earned and do not merit! You, pennyless! Famous equality and fraternization! Close union! Intimate attachment!"

"But, Jane, your aspirations after family ties and domestic happiness may be realized otherwise than by the means you contemplate: you may marry."

"Nonsense again! Marry! I don't want to marry, and never shall marry."

"That is saying too much: such hazardous affirmations are a proof of the excitement under which you labour."

"It is not saying too much: I know what I feel, and how averse are my inclinations to the bare thought of marriage. No one would take me for love; and I will not be regarded in the light of a mere money-speculation. And I do not want a stranger—unsympathizing, alien, different from me; I want my kindred: those with whom I have full fellow-feeling. Say again you will be my brother: when you uttered the words I was satisfied, happy;

repeat them, if you can, repeat them sincerely."

"I think I can. I know I have always loved my own sisters; and I know on what my affection for them is grounded,—respect for their worth, and admiration of their talents. You too have principle and mind: your tastes and habits resemble Diana's and Mary's; your presence is always agreeable to me; in your conversation I have already for some time found a salutary solace. I feel I can easily and naturally make room in my heart for you, as my third and youngest sister."

"Thank you: that contents me for to-night. Now you had better go; for if you stay longer, you will perhaps irritate me afresh by some mistrustful scruple."

"And the school, Miss Eyre? It must now be shut up, I suppose?"

"No. I will retain my post of mistress till you get a substitute."

He smiled approbation: we shook hands, and he took leave.

I need not narrate in detail the further struggles I had, and arguments I used, to get matters regarding the legacy settled as I wished. My task was a very hard one: but, as I was absolutely resolved—as my cousins saw at length that my mind was really and immutably fixed on making a just division of the property—as they must in their own hearts have felt the equity of the intention; and must, besides, have been innately conscious that in my place they would have done precisely what I wished to do—they yielded at length so far as to consent to put the affair to arbitration. The judges chosen were Mr. Oliver and an able lawyer: both coincided in my opinion: I carried my point. The instruments of transfer were drawn out: St. John, Diana, Mary, and I, each became possessed of a competency.

CHAPTER VIII.

IT was near Christmas by the time all was settled: the season of general holiday approached. I now closed Morton-school; taking care that the parting should not be barren on my side. Good fortune opens the hand as well as the heart wonderfully; and to give somewhat when we have largely received, is but to afford a vent to the unusual ebullition of the sensations. I had long felt with pleasure that many of my rustic scholars liked me, and when we parted, that consciousness was confirmed: they manifested their affection plainly and strongly. Deep was my gratification to find I had really a place in their unsophisticated hearts: I promised them that never a week should pass in future that I did not visit them, and give them an hour's teaching in their school.

Mr. Rivers came up, as,—having seen the

classes, now numbering sixty girls, file out
before me, and locked the door, — I stood
with the key in my hand, exchanging a few
words of special farewell with some half-dozen
of my best scholars: as decent, respectable,
modest, and well-informed young women as
could be found in the ranks of the British
peasantry. And that is saying a great deal;
for after all, the British peasantry are the
best taught, best mannered, most self-re-
specting of any in Europe: since those days I
have seen paysannes and Bäuerinnen; and the
best of them seemed to me ignorant, coarse,
and besotted, compared with my Morton
girls.

"Do you consider you have got your reward for a season of exertion?" asked Mr.
Rivers when they were gone. " Does not the
consciousness of having done some real good
in your day and generation give pleasure?"

" Doubtless."

" And you have only toiled a few months!
Would not a life devoted to the task of re-
generating your race be well spent?"

" Yes," I said; " but I could not go on for
ever so: I want to enjoy my own faculties
as well as to cultivate those of other people.
I must enjoy them now: don't recall either

my mind or body to the school; I am out
of it and disposed for full holiday."

He looked grave. "What now? What
sudden eagerness is this you evince? What
are you going to do?"

"To be active: as active as I can. And first
I must beg you to set Hannah at liberty, and
get somebody else to wait on you."

"Do you want her?"

"Yes, to go with me to Moor-House:
Diana and Mary will be at home in a week,
and I want to have everything in order against
their arrival."

"I understand: I thought you were for
flying off on some excursion. It is better so:
Hannah shall go with you."

"Tell her to be ready by to-morrow then;
and here is the school-room key: I will give
you the key of my cottage in the morning."

He took it. "You give it up very glee-
fully," said he: "I don't quite understand
your light-heartedness; because I cannot tell
what employment·you propose to yourself as
a substitute for the one you are relinquishing.
What aim, what purpose, what ambition in
life have you now?"

"My first aim will be to *clean down* (do you
comprehend the full force of the expression?)

to *clean down* Moor-House from chamber to cellar; my next to rub it up with beeswax, oil, and an indefinite number of cloths, till it glitters again; my third, to arrange every chair, table, bed, carpet, with mathematical precision; afterwards I shall go near to ruin you in coals and peat to keep up good fires in every room; and lastly, the two days preceding that on which your sisters are expected, will be devoted by Hannah and me to such a beating of eggs, sorting of currants, grating of spices, compounding of Christmas cakes, chopping up of materials for mince-pies, and solemnizing of other culinary rites, as words can convey but an inadequate notion of to the uninitiated like you. My purpose, in short, is to have all things in an absolutely perfect state of readiness for Diana and Mary, before next Thursday; and my ambition is to give them a beau ideal of a welcome when they come."

St. John smiled slightly: still he was dissatisfied.

"It is all very well for the present," said he: "but seriously, I trust that when the first flush of vivacity is over, you will look a little higher than domestic endearments and household joys."

"The best things the world has!" I interrupted.

"No, Jane, no : this world is not the scene
of fruition ; do not attempt to make it so :
nor of rest ; do not turn slothful."

"I mean, on the contrary, to be busy."

"Jane, I excuse you for the present : two
months' grace I allow you for the full enjoyment
of your new position, and for pleasing yourself
with this late-found charm of relationship ;
but *then*, I hope you will begin to look beyond
Moor-House and Morton, and sisterly society,
and the selfish calm and sensual comfort
of civilized affluence.   I hope your energies
will then once more trouble you with their
strength."

I looked at him with surprise.   "St. John,"
I said, "I think you are almost wicked to
talk so.   I am disposed to be as content as a
queen, and you try to stir me up to restlessness!   To what end?"

"To the end of turning to profit the talents
which God has committed to your keeping ;
and of which he will surely one day demand a
strict account.   Jane, I shall watch you closely
and anxiously—I warn you of that.   And try
to restrain the disproportionate fervour with
which you throw yourself into common-place

home pleasures. Don't cling so tenaciously to ties of the flesh; save your constancy and ardour for an adequate cause: forbear to waste them on trite transient objects. Do you hear, Jane?"

" Yes; just as if you were speaking Greek. I feel I have adequate cause to be happy, and I *will* be happy. Good-bye!"

Happy at Moor-House I was, and hard I worked; and so did Hannah: she was charmed to see how jovial I could be amidst the bustle of a house turned topsy-turvy—how I could brush, and dust, and clean, and cook. And really after a day or two of confusion worse confounded, it was delightful, by degrees, to invoke order from the chaos ourselves had made. I had previously taken a journey to S——, to purchase some new furniture: my cousins having given me carte blanche to effect what alterations I pleased, and a sum having been set aside for that purpose. The ordinary sitting-room and bed-rooms I left much as they were; for I knew Diana and Mary would derive more pleasure from seeing again the old homely tables, and chairs, and beds, than from the spectacle of the smartest innovations. Still some novelty was necessary, to give to their return the piquancy with which I wished

it to be invested. Dark handsome new carpets and curtains, an arrangement of some
carefully selected antique ornaments in porce-
lain and bronze, new coverings, and mirrors,
and dressing-cases for the toilet tables, answered the end: they looked fresh without being
glaring. A spare parlour and bed-room I
refurnished entirely, with old mahogany and
crimson upholstery: I laid canvass on the
passage, and carpets on the stairs. When all
was finished, I thought Moor-House as complete a model of bright modest snugness
within, as it was, at this season, a specimen
of wintry waste and desert dreariness without.

The eventful Thursday at length came.
They were expected about dark, and ere dusk,
fires were lit up stairs and below; the kitchen
was in perfect trim; Hannah and I were
dressed, and all was in readiness.

St. John arrived first. I had entreated him
to keep quite clear of the house till everything
was arranged: and, indeed, the bare idea of the
commotion, at once sordid and trivial, going
on within its walls sufficed to scare him to
estrangement. He found me in the kitchen,
watching the progress of certain cakes for tea,
then baking. Approaching the hearth, he
asked, " If I was at last satisfied with house-

maid's work?" I answered by inviting him to accompany me on a general inspection of the result of my labours. With some difficulty, I got him to make the tour of the house. He just looked in at the doors I opened; and when he had wandered up stairs and down stairs, he said I must have gone through a great deal of fatigue and trouble to have effected such considerable changes in so short a time: but not a syllable did he utter indicating pleasure in the improved aspect of his abode.

This silence damped me. I thought perhaps the alterations had disturbed some old associations he valued. I inquired whether this was the case: no doubt in a somewhat crest-fallen tone.

" Not at all; he had, on the contrary, remarked that I had scrupulously respected every association: he feared, indeed, I must have bestowed more thought on the matter than it was worth. How many minutes, for instance, had I devoted to studying the arrangement of this very room?—By-the-bye, could I tell him where such a book was?"

I showed him the volume on the shelf: he took it down; and withdrawing to his accustomed window recess, he began to read it.

Now, I did not like this, reader. St. John was a good man; but I began to feel he had spoken truth of himself, when he said he was hard and cold. The humanities and amenities of life had no attraction for him—its peaceful enjoyments no charm. Literally, he lived only to aspire — after what was good and great, certainly: but still he would never rest; nor approve of others resting round him. As I looked at his lofty forehead, still and pale as a white stone—at his fine lineaments fixed in study—I comprehended all at once that he would hardly make a good husband: that it would be a trying thing to be his wife. I understood, as by inspiration, the nature of his love for Miss Oliver: I agreed with him that it was but a love of the senses. I comprehended how he should despise himself for the feverish influence it exercised over him; how he should wish to stifle and destroy it; how he should mistrust its ever conducing permanently to his happiness, or hers. I saw he was of the material from which nature hews her heroes—Christian and Pagan—her lawgivers, her statesmen, her conquerors: a steadfast bulwark for great interests to rest upon; but, at the fireside, too often a cold cumbrous column, gloomy and out of place.

" This parlour is not his sphere," I reflected :
" the Himalayan ridge, or Caffre bush, even the
plague-cursed Guinea coast swamp, would suit
him better. Well may he eschew the calm of
domestic life; it is not his element: there his
faculties stagnate — they cannot develope or
appear to advantage. It is in scenes of strife
and danger—where courage is proved, and
energy exercised, and fortitude tasked—that he
will speak and move, the leader and superior.
A merry child would have the advantage of
him on this hearth. He is right to choose a
missionary's career—I see it now."

" They are coming! they are coming!"
cried Hannah, throwing open the parlour
door. At the same moment old Carlo barked
joyfully. Out I ran. It was now dark; but a
rumbling of wheels was audible. Hannah
soon had a lantern lit. The vehicle had
stopped at the wicket; the driver opened the
door: first one well-known form, then another,
stepped out. In a minute I had my face under
their bonnets, in contact, first with Mary's
soft cheek, then with Diana's flowing curls.
They laughed — kissed me — then Hannah:
patted Carlo, who was half wild with delight,
asked eagerly if all was well; and being
assured in the affirmative, hastened into the
house.

They were stiff with their long and jolting drive from Whitcross, and chilled with the frosty night air; but their pleasant countenances expanded to the cheering fire light. While the driver and Hannah brought in the boxes, they demanded St. John. At this moment he advanced from the parlour. They both threw their arms round his neck at once. He gave each one quiet kiss, said in a low tone a few words of welcome, stood awhile to be talked to, and then, intimating that he supposed they would soon rejoin him in the parlour, withdrew there as to a place of refuge.

I had lit their candles to go up stairs, but Diana had first to give hospitable orders respecting the driver; this done, both followed me. They were delighted with the renovation and decoration of their rooms; with the new drapery, and fresh carpets, and rich tinted china vases: they expressed their gratification ungrudgingly. I had the pleasure of feeling that my arrangements met their wishes exactly; and that what I had done added a vivid charm to their joyous return home.

Sweet was that evening. My cousins, full of exhilaration, were so eloquent in narrative and comment, that their fluency covered St. John's taciturnity: he was sincerely glad to see his sisters; but in their glow of fervour and flow of joy he could not sympathize. The event of the day—that is, the return of Diana and Mary—pleased him; but the accompaniments of that event, the glad tumult, the garrulous glee of reception, irked him: I saw he wished the calmer morrow was come. In the very meridian of the night's enjoyment, about an hour after tea, a rap was heard at the door. Hannah entered, with the intimation that " a poor lad was come, at that unlikely time, to fetch Mr. Rivers to see his mother, who was drawing away."

" Where does she live, Hannah ?"

" Clear up at Whitcross Brow, almost four miles off; and moor and moss all the way."

" Tell him I will go."

" I'm sure, sir, you had better not. It's the worst road to travel after dark that can be: there's no track at all over the bog. And then it is such a bitter night—the keenest wind you ever felt. You had better send word, sir, that you will be there in the morning."

But he was already in the passage, putting on his cloak; and without one objection, one murmur, he departed. It was then nine o'clock: he did not return till midnight.

Starved and tired enough he was: but he looked happier than when he set out. He had performed an act of duty; made an exertion; felt his own strength to do and deny, and was on better terms with himself.

I am afraid the whole of the ensuing week tried his patience. It was Christmas week: we took to ·no settled employment, but spent it in a sort of merry domestic dissipation. The air of the moors, the freedom of home, the dawn of prosperity, acted on Diana's and Mary's spirits like some life-giving elixir: they were gay from morning till noon, and from noon till night. They could always talk; and their discourse, witty, pithy, original, had such charms for me, that I preferred listening to, and sharing in it, to doing anything else. St. John did not rebuke our vivacity; but he escaped from it: he was seldom in the house: his parish was large, the population scattered, and he found daily business in visiting the sick and poor in its different districts.

One morning, at breakfast, Diana, after looking a little pensive for some minutes, asked him "If his plans were yet unchanged?"

"Unchanged and unchangeable," was the reply. And he proceeded to inform us that

his departure from England was now definitively fixed for the ensuing year.

"And Rosamond Oliver?" suggested Mary:
the words seeming to escape her lips involuntarily; for no sooner had she uttered them,
than she made a gesture as if wishing to recall
them. St. John had a book in his hand—it
was his unsocial custom to read at meals—he
closed it, and looked up.

"Rosamond Oliver," said he, "is about to
be married to Mr. Granby; one of the best
connected and most estimable residents in
S——, grandson and heir to Sir Frederic
Granby: I had the intelligence from her father
yesterday."

His sisters looked at each other, and at me; we
all three looked at him: he was serene as glass.

"The match must have been got up hastily,"
said Diana: "they cannot have known each
other long."

"But two months: they met in October
at the county ball at S——. But where there
are no obstacles to a union, as in the present
case, where the connection is in every point
desirable, delays are unnecessary: they will
be married as soon as S—— Place, which Sir
Frederic gives up to them, can be refitted for
their reception."

The first time I found St. John alone after this communication, I felt tempted to inquire if the event distressed him : but he seemed so little to need sympathy, that, so far from venturing to offer him more, I experienced some shame at the recollection of what I had already hazarded.   Besides, I was out of practice in talking to him : his reserve was again frozen over, and my frankness was congealed beneath it.   He had not kept his promise of treating me like his sisters; he continually made little, chilling differences between us, which did not at all tend to the development of cordiality : in short, now that I was acknowledged his kinswoman, and lived under the same roof with him, I felt the distance between us to be far greater than when he had known me only as the village schoolmistress. When I remembered how far I had once been admitted to his confidence, I could hardly comprehend his present frigidity.

Such being the case, I felt not a little surprised when he raised his head suddenly from the desk over which he was stooping, and said :

" You see, Jane, the battle is fought and the victory won."

Startled at being thus addressed, I did not immediately reply ; after a moment's hesitation I answered :—

"But are you sure you are not in the position of those conquerors whose triumphs have cost them too dear? Would not such another ruin you?"

"I think not; and if I were, it does not much signify: I shall never be called upon to contend for such another. The event of the conflict is decisive: my way is now clear; I thank God for it!" So saying, he returned to his papers and his silence.

As our mutual happiness (*i. e.* Diana's, Mary's, and mine) settled into a quieter character, and we resumed our usual habits and regular studies, St. John stayed more at home: he sat with us in the same room, sometimes for hours together. While Mary drew, Diana pursued a course of Encyclopædic reading she had (to my awe and amazement) undertaken, and I fagged away at German, he pondered a mystic lore of his own: that of some Eastern tongue, the acquisition of which he thought necessary to his plans.

Thus engaged, he appeared, sitting in his own recess, quiet and absorbed enough; but that blue eye of his had a habit of leaving the outlandish-looking grammar, and wandering over, and sometimes fixing upon us, his fellow-students, with a curious intensity of observation:

if caught, it would be instantly withdrawn;
yet ever and anon, it returned searchingly to
our table. I wondered what it meant: I
wondered, too, at the punctual satisfaction he
never failed to exhibit on an occasion that
seemed to me of small moment, namely,—my
weekly visit to Morton school; and still more
was I puzzled when, if the day was unfavourable, if there was snow, or rain, or high wind,
and his sisters urged me not to go, he would
invariably make light of their solicitude, and
encourage me to accomplish the task without
regard to the elements.

"Jane is not such a weakling as you would
make her," he would say; "she can bear a
mountain blast, or a shower, or a few flakes of
snow, as well as any of us. Her constitution
is both sound and elastic;—better calculated
to endure variations of climate than many more
robust."

And when I returned, sometimes a good
deal tired, and not a little weather-beaten, I
never dared complain, because I saw that to
murmur would be to vex him: on all occasions
fortitude pleased him; the reverse was a
special annoyance.

One afternoon, however, I got leave to stay
at home, because I really had a cold. His

sisters were gone to Morton in my stead: I sat reading Schiller; he, deciphering his crabbed Oriental scrolls. As I exchanged a translation for an exercise, I happened to look his way: there I found myself under the influence of the ever-watchful blue eye. How long it had been searching me through and through, and over and over, I cannot tell: so keen was it, and yet so cold, I felt for the moment super-stitious—as if I were sitting in the room with something uncanny.

"Jane, what are you doing?"

"Learning German."

"I want you to give up German, and learn Hindostanee."

"You are not in earnest?"

"In such earnest that I must have it so: and I will tell you why."

He then went on to explain that Hindostanee was the language he was himself at present studying; that as he advanced, he was apt to forget the commencement; that it would assist him greatly to have a pupil with whom he might again and again go over the elements, and so fix them thoroughly in his mind; that his choice had hovered for some time between me and his sisters; but that he had fixed it on me, because he saw I could sit at a task the longest of the three. Would I do him this favour? I should not, perhaps, have to make the sacrifice long; as it wanted now barely three months to his departure.

St. John was not a man to be lightly refused: you felt that every impression made on him, either for pain or pleasure, was deepgraved and permanent. I consented. When Diana and Mary returned, the former found her scholar transferred from her to her brother: she laughed; and both she and Mary agreed that St. John should never have persuaded them to such a step. He answered, quietly:—

"I knew it."

I found him a very patient, very forbearing, and yet an exacting master: he expected me to do a great deal; and when I fulfilled his expectations he, in his own way, fully testified his approbation. By degrees, he acquired a certain influence over me that took away my liberty of mind: his praise and notice were more restraining than his indifference. I could no longer talk or laugh freely when he was by; because a tiresomely importunate instinct reminded me that vivacity (at least in me) was distasteful to him. I was so fully aware that only serious moods and occupations were acceptable; that in his presence every effort to sustain or follow any other, became vain: I fell under a freezing spell. When he said " go," I went; " come," I came; " do this," I did it. But I did not love my servitude: I wished, many a time, he had continued to neglect me.

One evening when, at bed-time, his sisters and I stood round him, bidding him good-night, he kissed each of them, as was his custom; and, as was equally his custom, he gave me his hand. Diana, who chanced to be in a frolicksome humour (*she* was not painfully controlled by his will; for hers, in another way, was as strong), exclaimed :—

" St. John! you used to call Jane your third sister, but you don't treat her as such: you should kiss her too."

She pushed me towards him. I thought Diana very provoking, and felt uncomfortably confused; and while I was thus thinking and feeling, St. John bent his head, his Greek face was brought to a level with mine, his eyes questioned my eyes piercingly—he kissed me. There are no such things as marble kisses, or ice kisses, or I should say, my ecclesiastical cousin's salute belonged to one of these classes; but there may be experiment kisses, and his was an experiment kiss. When given, he viewed me to learn the result; it was not striking: I am sure I did not blush; perhaps I might have turned a little pale, for I felt as if this kiss were a seal affixed to my fetters. He never omitted the ceremony afterwards, and the gravity and quiescence with which I underwent it, seemed to invest it for him with a certain charm.

As for me, I daily wished more to please him: but to do so, I felt daily more and more that I must disown half my nature, stifle half my faculties, wrest my tastes from their original bent, force myself to the adoption of pursuits for which I had no natural vocation. He wanted to train me to an elevation I could never reach: it racked me hourly to aspire to the standard he uplifted. The thing was as impossible as to mould my irregular features to his correct and classic pattern, to give to my changeable green eyes the sea blue tint and solemn lustre of his own.

Not his ascendancy alone, however, held me in thrall at present. Of late it had been easy enough for me to look sad: a cankering evil sat at my heart and drained my happiness at its source—the evil of suspense.

Perhaps you think I had forgotten Mr.

Rochester, reader, amidst these changes of place and fortune. Not for a moment. His idea was still with me; because it was not a vapour sunshine could disperse; nor a sand-traced effigy storms could wash away: it was a name graven on a tablet, fated to last as long as the marble it inscribed. The craving to know what had become of him followed me everywhere: when I was at Morton, I re-entered my cottage every evening to think of that; and now at Moor-House, I sought my bedroom each night to brood over it.

In the course of my necessary correspondence with Mr Briggs about the will, I had inquired if he knew anything of Mr. Rochester's present residence and state of health: but, as St. John had conjectured, he was quite ignorant of all concerning him. I then wrote to Mrs. Fairfax, entreating information on the subject. I had calculated with certainty on this step answering my end: I felt sure it would elicit an early answer. I was astonished when a fortnight passed without reply; but when two months wore away, and day after day the post arrived and brought nothing for me, I fell a prey to the keenest anxiety.

I wrote again: there was a chance of my first letter having missed. Renewed hope fol-

lowed renewed effort; it shone like the former
for some weeks, then, like it, it faded, flick-
ered: not a line, not a word reached me.
When half a year wasted in vain expectancy,
my hope died out; and then I felt dark indeed.

A fine spring shone round me, which I could
not enjoy. Summer approached; Diana tried
to cheer me: she said I looked ill, and wished
to accompany me to the sea-side. This St.
John opposed; he said I did not want dissipation, I wanted employment: my present
life was too purposeless, I required an aim;
and, I suppose, by way of supplying deficiencies, he prolonged still further my lessons
in Hindostanee, and grew more urgent in
requiring their accomplishment: and I, like
a fool, never thought of resisting him—I could
not resist him.

One day I had come to my studies in lower
spirits than usual; the ebb was occasioned by a
poignantly felt disappointment: Hannah had
told me in the morning there was a letter for
me, and when I went down to take it, almost
certain that the long looked-for tidings were
vouchsafed me at last, I found only an un-
important note from Mr. Briggs on business.
The bitter check had wrung from me some
tears; and now as I sat poring over the crab-

bed characters and flourishing tropes of an Indian scribe, my eyes filled again.

St. John called me to his side to read; in attempting to do this my voice failed me: words were lost in sobs. He and I were the only occupants of the parlour: Diana was practising her music in the drawing-room, Mary was gardening—it was a very fine May-day, clear, sunny, and breezy. My companion expressed no surprise at this emotion, nor did he question me as to its cause; he only said:—

"We will wait a few minutes, Jane, till you are more composed. And while I smothered the paroxysm with all haste, he sat calm and patient, leaning on his desk and looking like a physician watching with the eye of science an expected and fully-understood crisis in a patient's malady. Having stifled my sobs, wiped my eyes, and muttered something about not being very well that morning, I resumed my task, and succeeded in completing it. St. John put away my books and his, locked his desk, and said:—

"Now, Jane, you shall take a walk; and with me."

"I will call Diana and Mary."

"No. I want only one companion this

morning, and that must be you: put on your things; go out by the kitchen door; take the road towards the head of Marsh-Glen: I will join you in a moment."

I know no medium: I never in my life have known any medium in my dealings with positive, hard characters, antagonistic to my own, between absolute submission and determined revolt. I have always faithfully observed the one, up to the very moment of bursting, sometimes with volcanic vehemence, into the other; and as neither present circumstances warranted, nor my present mood inclined me to mutiny, I observed careful obedience to St. John's directions; and in ten minutes I was treading the wild track of the glen, side by side with him.

The breeze was from the west: it came over the hills, sweet with scents of heath and rush; the sky was of stainless blue; the stream descending the ravine, swelled with past spring rains, poured along plentiful and clear, catching golden gleams from the sun, and sapphire tints from the firmament. As we advanced and left the track, we trod a soft turf, mossy fine and emerald green, minutely enamelled with a tiny white flower, and spangled with a star-like yellow blossom: the hills, meantime, shut us quite in; for the glen, towards its head, wound to their very core.

"Let us rest here," said St. John, as we reached the first stragglers of a battalion of rocks, guarding a sort of pass, beyond which the beck rushed down, a waterfall; and where, still a little further, the mountain shook off turf and flower, had only heath for raiment, and crag for gem—where it exaggerated the wild to the savage, and exchanged the fresh for the frowning—where it guarded the forlorn hope of solitude, and a last refuge for silence.

I took a seat: St. John stood near me. He looked up the pass and down the hollow; his glance wandered away with the stream, and returned to traverse the unclouded heaven which coloured it: he removed his hat, let the breeze stir his hair and kiss his brow. He seemed in communion with the genius of the haunt: with his eye he bade farewell to something.

"And I shall see it again," he said aloud, "in dreams, when I sleep by the Ganges: and again, in a more remote hour—when another slumber overcomes me—on the shore of a darker stream."

Strange words of a strange love! An austere patriot's passion for his fatherland! He sat down: for half an hour we never

spoke; neither he to me nor I to him: tha
interval past, he recommenced :—

"Jane, I go in six weeks; I have taken my
berth in an East Indiaman which sails on the
twentieth of June."

"God will protect you; for you have undertaken his work," I answered.

"Yes," said he, "there is my glory and joy.
I am the servant of an infallible master. I am
not going out under human guidance, subject
to the defective laws and erring control of my
feeble fellow-worms: my king, my lawgiver,
my captain, is the All-perfect. It seems
strange to me that all round me do not burn to
enlist under the same banner—to join in the
same enterprise."

"All have not your powers; and it would be
folly for the feeble to wish to march with the
strong."

"I do not speak to the feeble, or think of
them: I address only such as are worthy of
the work, and competent to accomplish it."

"Those are few in number, and difficult to
discover."

"You say truly: but when found, it is right
to stir them up—to urge and exhort them to
the effort—to show them what their gifts are,
and why they were given—to speak Heaven's

message in their ear,—to offer them, direct from God, a place in the ranks of his chosen."

" If they are really qualified for the task, will not their own hearts be the first to inform them of it?"

I felt as if an awful charm was framing round and gathering over me: I trembled to hear some fatal word spoken which would at once declare and rivet the spell.

" And what does *your* heart say?" demanded St. John.

" My heart is mute,—my heart is mute," I answered, struck and thrilled.

" Then I must speak for it," continued the deep, relentless voice. " Jane, come with me to India: come as my help-meet and fellow-labourer."

The glen and sky spun round: the hills heaved! It was as if I had heard a summons from Heaven—as if a visionary messenger, like him of Macedonia, had enounced " Come over and help us!" But I was no apostle,—I could not behold the herald,—I could not receive his call.

" Oh, St. John!" I cried, " have some mercy!"

I appealed to one, who, in the discharge of

what he believed his duty, knew neither mercy
nor remorse. He continued :—

" God and nature intended you for a missionary's wife. It is not personal, but mental
endowments they have given you: you are
formed for labour, not for love. A missionary's wife you must—shall be. You shall be
mine: I claim you—not for my pleasure, but
for my Sovereign's service."

" I am not fit for it : I have no vocation," I
said.

He had calculated on these first objections :
he was not irritated by them. Indeed, as he
leaned back against the crag behind him,
folded his arms on his chest, and fixed his
countenance, I saw he was prepared for a
long and trying opposition, and had taken in
a stock of patience to last him to its close—
resolved, however, that that close should be
conquest for him.

" Humility, Jane," said he, " is the ground-
work of Christian virtues : you say right that
you are not fit for the work. Who is fit for
it? Or who, that ever was truly called, believed himself worthy of the summons? I,
for instance, am but dust and ashes. With
St. Paul I acknowledge myself the chiefest of
sinners : but I do not suffer this sense of my

personal vileness to daunt me. I know my Leader: that He is just as well as mighty; and while He has chosen a feeble instrument to perform a great task, He will, from the boundless stores of His providence, supply the inadequacy of the means to the end. Think like me, Jane—trust like me. It is the Rock of Ages I ask you to lean on: do not doubt but it will bear the weight of your human weakness."

" I do not understand a missionary life: I have never studied missionary labours."

" There, I, humble as I am, can give you the aid you want: I can set you your task from hour to hour; stand by you always; help you from moment to moment. This I could do in the beginning: soon (for I know your powers) you would be as strong and apt as myself, and would not require my help."

" But my powers—where are they for this undertaking? I do not feel them. Nothing speaks or stirs in me while you talk. I am sensible of no light kindling—no life quickening—no voice counselling or cheering. Oh, I wish I could make you see how much my mind is at this moment like a rayless dungeon, with one shrinking fear fettered in its depths

—the fear of being persuaded by you to attempt what I cannot accomplish!"

"I have an answer for you—hear it. I have watched you ever since we first met: I have made you my study for ten months. I have proved you in that time by sundry tests: and what have I seen and elicited? In the village school I found you could perform well, punctually, uprightly, labour uncongenial to your habits and inclinations; I saw you could perform it with capacity and tact: you could win while you controlled. In the calm with which you learnt you had become suddenly rich, I read a mind clear of the vice of Demas: —lucre had no undue power over you. In the resolute readiness with which you cut your wealth into four shares, keeping but one to yourself, and relinquishing the three others to the claim of abstract justice, I recognised a soul that revelled in the flame and excitement of sacrifice. In the tractability with which, at my wish, you forsook a study in which you were interested, and adopted another, because it interested me; in the untiring assiduity with which you have since persevered in it— in the unflagging energy and unshaken temper with which you have met its difficulties—I acknowledge the complement of the qualities

I seek. Jane, you are docile, diligent, disinterested, faithful, constant, and courageous; very gentle, and very heroic: cease to mistrust yourself—I can trust you unreservedly. As a conductress of Indian schools, and a helper amongst Indian women, your assistance will be to me invaluable."

My iron shroud contracted round me: persuasion advanced with slow sure step. Shut my eyes as I would, these last words of his succeeded in making the way, which had seemed blocked up, comparatively clear. My work, which had appeared so vague, so hopelessly diffuse, condensed itself as he proceeded, and assumed a definite form under his shaping hand. He waited for an answer. I demanded a quarter of an hour to think, before I again hazarded a reply.

"Very willingly," he rejoined; and rising, he strode a little distance up the pass, threw himself down on a swell of heath, and there lay still.

"I *can* do what he wants me to do: I am forced to see and acknowledge that," I meditated—"that is, if life be spared me. But I feel mine is not the existence to be long protracted under an Indian sun.—What then? He does not care for that: when my time came to die he would resign me, in all serenity and sanctity, to the God who gave me. The case is very plain before me. In leaving England, I should leave a loved but empty land—Mr. Rochester is not there: and if he were, what is, what can that ever be to me? My business is to live without him now: nothing so absurd, so weak as to drag on from day to day, as if I were waiting some impossible change in circumstances, which might reunite me to him. Of course (as St. John once said) I must seek another interest in life to replace the one lost: is not the occupation he now offers me truly the most glorious man can adopt or God assign? Is it not, by its noble cares and sublime results, the one best calculated to fill the void left by uptorn affections and demolished hopes? I believe I must say, yes—and yet I shudder. Alas! If I join St. John, I abandon half myself: if I go to India, I go to premature death. And how will the interval between leaving England for India, and India for the grave, be filled? Oh, I know well! That, too, is very clear to my vision. By straining to satisfy St. John till my sinews ache, I *shall* satisfy him—to the finest central point and farthest outward circle of his expectations. If I *do* go with him—if I *do* make the sacrifice he urges,

I will make it absolutely: I will throw all on the altar—heart, vitals, the entire victim. He will never love me; but he shall approve me: I will show him energies he has not yet seen, resources he has never suspected. Yes: I can work as hard as he can; and with as little grudging.

"Consent, then, to his demand is possible: but for one item—one dreadful item. It is—that he asks me to be his wife, and has no more of a husband's heart for me than that frowning giant of a rock, down which the stream is foaming in yonder gorge. He prizes me as a soldier would a good weapon; and that is all. Unmarried to him, this would never grieve me; but can I let him complete his calculations—coolly put into practice his plans—go through the wedding ceremony? Can I receive from him the bridal ring, endure all the forms of love (which I doubt not he would scrupulously observe) and know that the spirit was quite absent? Can I bear the consciousness that every endearment he bestows is a sacrifice made on principle? No: such a martyrdom would be monstrous. I will never undergo it: As his sister, I might accompany him—not as his wife: I will tell him so."

I looked towards the knoll: there he lay,

still as a prostrate column; his face turned
to me: his eye beaming watchful, and keen.
He started to his feet and approached me.

"I am ready to go to India, if I may go
free."

"Your answer requires a commentary," he
said; "it is not clear."

"You have hitherto been my adopted
brother: I, your adopted sister; let us continue as such: you and I had better not
marry."

He shook his head. "Adopted fraternity
will not do in this case. If you were my real
sister it would be different: I should take you,
and seek no wife. But, as it is, either our
union must be consecrated and sealed by marriage, or it cannot exist: practical obstacles
oppose themselves to any other plan. Do you
see it, Jane? Consider a moment—your
strong sense will guide you."

I did consider: and still my sense, such as it
was, directed me only to the fact that we did
not love each other as man and wife should;
and therefore it inferred we ought not to
marry. I said so. "St. John," I returned,
"I regard you as a brother—you, me as a
sister: so let us continue."

"We cannot—we cannot," he answered with,

short, sharp determination: "it would not do. You have said you will go with me to India: remember—you have said that."

"Conditionally."

"Well—well. To the main point—the departure with me from England, the co-operation with me in my future labours—you do not object. You have already as good as put your hand to the plough: you are too consistent to withdraw it. You have but one end to keep in view—how the work you have undertaken can best be done. Simplify your complicated interests, feelings, thoughts, wishes, aims; merge all considerations in one purpose: that of fulfilling with effect—with power—the mission of your great Master. To do so, you must have a coadjutor—not a brother; that is a loose tie: but a husband. I, too, do not want a sister: a sister might any day be taken from me. I want a wife: the sole helpmeet I can influence efficiently in life, and retain absolutely till death."

I shuddered as he spoke: I felt his influence in my marrow—his hold on my limbs.

"Seek one elsewhere than in me, St. John: seek one fitted to you."

"One fitted to my purpose, you mean—fitted to my vocation. Again I tell you it is not the insignificant private individual—the mere man, with the man's selfish senses—I wish to mate : it is the missionary."

" And I will give the missionary my energies—it is all he wants—but not myself : that would be only adding the husk and shell to the kernel. For them he has no use : I retain them."

" You cannot—you ought not. Do you think God will be satisfied with half an oblation? Will He accept a mutilated sacrifice? It is the cause of God I advocate : it is under His standard I enlist you. I cannot accept on His behalf a divided allegiance : it must be entire."

" Oh ! I will give my heart to God," I said. " *You* do not want it."

I will not swear, reader, that there was not something of repressed sarcasm both in the tone in which I uttered this sentence, and in the feeling that accompanied it. I had silently feared St. John till now, because I had not understood him. He had held me in awe, because he had held me in doubt. How much of him was saint, how much mortal, I could not heretofore tell ; but revelations were being made in this conference : the analysis of his nature was proceeding before my eyes. I saw his fallibilities : I comprehended them. I understood that, sitting there where I did, on the bank of heath, and with that handsome form before me, I sat at the feet of a man, erring as I. The veil fell from his hardness and despotism. Having felt in him the presence of these qualities, I felt his imperfection, and took courage. I was with an equal—one with whom I might argue—one whom, if I saw good, I might resist.

He was silent after I had uttered the last sentence, and I presently risked an upward glance at his countenance. His eye, bent on me, expressed at once stern surprise and keen inquiry. " Is she sarcastic, and sarcastic to *me ?*" it seemed to say. " What does this signify ?"

" Do not let us forget that this is a solemn matter," he said, ere long ; " one of which we may neither think nor talk lightly without sin. I trust, Jane, you are in earnest when you say you will give your heart to God: it is all I want. Once wrench your heart from man, and fix it on your Maker, the advancement of that Maker's spiritual kingdom on earth will be your chief delight and endeavour: you will be ready to do at once whatever furthers that end. You will see what impetus would be

given to your efforts and mine by our physical
and mental union in marriage: the only union
that gives a character of permanent conformity
to the destinies and designs of human beings;
and, passing over all minor caprices—all trivial
difficulties and delicacies of feeling—all scruple
about the degree, kind, strength, or tenderness
of mere personal inclination—you will hasten
to enter into that union at once."

"Shall I?" I said briefly; and I looked at
his features, beautiful in their harmony, but
strangely formidable in their still severity: at
his brow, commanding but not open; at his
eyes, bright, and deep, and searching, but never
soft; at his tall, imposing figure; and fancied
myself in idea, *his wife*. Oh! it would never
do! As his curate, his comrade, all would be
right: I would cross oceans with him in that
capacity; toil under eastern suns, in Asian
deserts with him in that office; admire and
emulate his courage, and devotion, and vigour;
accommodate quietly to his masterhood; smile
undisturbed at his ineradicable ambition; dis-
criminate the Christian from the man; profoundly esteem the one, and freely forgive the
other. I should suffer often, no doubt, attached
to him only in this capacity: my body would
be under rather a stringent yoke, but my

heart and mind would be free. I should still have my unblighted self to turn to: my natural unenslaved feelings with which to communicate in moments of loneliness. There would be recesses in my mind which would be only mine, to which he never came; and sentiments growing there fresh and sheltered, which his austerity could never blight, nor his measured warrior-march trample down: but as his wife—at his side always, and always restrained, and always checked—forced to keep the fire of my nature continually low, to compel it to burn inwardly and never utter a cry, though the imprisoned flame consumed vital after vital—*this* would be unendurable.

"St. John!" I exclaimed, when I had got so far in my meditation.

"Well?" he answered, icily.

"I repeat: I freely consent to go with you as your fellow-missionary; but not as your wife: I cannot marry you and become a part of you."

"A part of me you must become," he answered, steadily; "otherwise the whole bargain is void. How can I, a man not yet thirty, take out with me to India a girl of nineteen, unless she is married to me? How can we be for ever together—sometimes in solitudes, sometimes amidst savage tribes—and unwed?"

"Very well," I said shortly; "under the circumstances; quite as well as if I were either your real sister; or a man and a clergyman, like yourself."

"It is known that you are not my sister; I cannot introduce you as such: to attempt it would be to fasten injurious suspicions on us both. And for the rest, though you have a man's vigorous brain, you have a woman's heart, and—it would not do."

"It would do," I affirmed, with some disdain, "perfectly well. I have a woman's heart; but not where you are concerned: for you I have only a comrade's constancy; a fellow-soldier's frankness, fidelity, fraternity, if you like; a neophyte's respect and submission to his hierophant: nothing more—don't fear."

"It is what I want," he said, speaking to himself; "it is just what I want. And there are obstacles in the way: they must be hewn down. Jane, you would not repent marrying me; be certain of that: we *must* be married. I repeat it: there is no other way; and undoubtedly enough of love would follow upon marriage to render the union right even in your eyes."

" I scorn your idea of love," I could not help saying ; as I rose up and stood before him, leaning my back against the rock. " I scorn the counterfeit sentiment you offer : yes, St. John, and I scorn you when you offer it."

He looked at me fixedly : compressing his well-cut lips while he did so. Whether he was incensed or surprised, or what, it was not easy to tell : he could command his countenance thoroughly.

" I scarcely expected to hear that expression from you," he said : " I think I have done and uttered nothing to deserve scorn."

I was touched by his gentle tone, and over-awed by his high, calm mien.

" Forgive me the words, St. John : but it is your own fault that I have been roused to speak so unguardedly. You have introduced a topic on which our natures are at variance—a topic we should never discuss : the very name of love is an apple of discord between us—if the reality were required, what should we do ? How should we feel ? My dear cousin, abandon your scheme of marriage—forget it."

" No," said he ; " it is a long-cherished scheme, and the only one which can secure my great end : but I shall urge you no further at present. To-morrow I leave home for

Cambridge: I have many friends there to whom I should wish to say farewell. I shall be absent a fortnight—take that space of time to consider my offer: and do not forget that if you reject it, it is not me you deny, but God. Through my means, He opens to you a noble career: as my wife only can you enter upon it. Refuse to be my wife, and you limit yourself for ever to a track of selfish ease and barren obscurity. Tremble, lest in that case you should be numbered with those who have denied the faith and are worse than infidels!"

He had done. Turning from me, he once more—

> " Looked to river, looked to hill :"

But this time his feelings were all pent in his heart: I was not worthy to hear them uttered. As I walked by his side homeward, I read well in his iron silence all he felt towards me: the disappointment of an austere and despotic nature, which has met resistance where it expected submission—the disapprobation of a cool, inflexible judgment, which has detected in another feelings and views in which it has no power to sympathize: in short, as a man, he would have wished to coerce me into obedience: it was only as a sincere Christian he bore so patiently with my perversity, and allowed so long a space for reflection and repentance.

That night, after he had kissed his sisters, he thought proper to forget even to shake hands with me; but left the room in silence. I—who, though I had no love, had much friendship for him—was hurt by the marked omission: so much hurt that tears started to my eyes.

"I see you and St. John have been quarrelling, Jane," said Diana, "during your walk on the moor. But go after him; he is now lingering in the passage, expecting you—he will make it up."

I have not much pride under such circumstances: I would always rather be happy than dignified; and I ran after him—he stood at the foot of the stairs.

"Good-night, St. John," said I.

"Good-night, Jane," he replied, calmly.

"Then shake hands," I added.

What a cold, loose touch he impressed on my fingers! He was deeply displeased by what had occurred that day: cordiality would not warm, nor tears move him. No happy reconciliation was to be had with him—no cheering smile or generous word: but still the

Christian was patient and placid; and when I asked him if he forgave me, he answered that he was not in the habit of cherishing the remembrance of vexation; that he had nothing to forgive; not having been offended.

And with that answer, he left me. I would much rather he had knocked me down.

CHAPTER IX.

HE did not leave for Cambridge the next day,
as he had said he would. He deferred his departure a whole week; and during that time he
made me feel what severe punishment a good,
yet stern, a conscientious, yet implacable man
can inflict on one who has offended him.
Without one overt act of hostility, one up-
braiding word, he contrived to impress me
momently with the conviction that I was put
beyond the pale of his favour.

Not that St. John harboured a spirit of un-
christian vindictiveness—not that he would
have injured a hair of my head, if it had been
fully in his power to do so. Both by nature
and principle he was superior to the mean
gratification of vengeance: he had forgiven
me for saying I scorned him and his love, but
he had not forgotten the words; and as long as
he and I lived he never would forget them.

I saw by his look, when turned to me, that they were always written on the air between me and him: whenever I spoke, they sounded in my voice to his ear; and their echo toned every answer he gave me.

He did not abstain from conversing with me: he even called me as usual each morning to join him at his desk; and I fear the corrupt man within him had a pleasure unimparted to, and unshared by, the pure Christian, in evincing with what skill he could, while acting and speaking apparently just as usual, extract from every deed and every phrase the spirit of interest and approval which had formerly communicated a certain austere charm to his language and manner. To me, he was in reality become no longer flesh, but marble: his eye was a cold, bright, blue gem; his tongue, a speaking instrument—nothing more.

All this was torture to me—refined, lingering torture. It kept up a slow fire of indignation, and a trembling trouble of grief, which harassed and crushed me altogether. I felt how—if I were his wife—this good man, pure as the deep sunless source, could soon kill me; without drawing from my veins a single drop of blood, or receiving on his own crystal conscience the faintest stain of crime. Especially

I felt this, when I made any attempt to propitiate him. No ruth met my ruth. *He* experienced no suffering from estrangement—no yearning after reconciliation; and though, more than once, my fast falling tears blistered the page over which we both bent, they produced no more effect on him than if his heart had been really a matter of stone or metal. To his sisters, meantime, he was somewhat kinder than usual: as if afraid that mere coldness would not sufficiently convince me how completely I was banished and banned, he added the force of contrast; and this I am sure he did, not by malice, but on principle.

The night before he left home, happening to see him walking in the garden about sunset, and remembering, as I looked at him, that this man, alienated as he now was, had once saved my life, and that we were near relations, I was moved to make a last attempt to regain his friendship. I went out and approached him, as he stood leaning over the little gate : I spoke to the point at once.

" St. John, I am unhappy, because you are still angry with me. Let us be friends."

" I hope we are friends," was the unmoved reply; while he still watched the rising of the moon, which he had been contemplating as I approached.

" No, St. John, we are not friends as we were. You know that."

" Are we not? That is wrong. For my part, I wish you no ill and all good."

"I believe you, St. John; for I am sure you are incapable of wishing any one ill: but, as I am your kinswoman, I should desire somewhat more of affection than that sort of general philanthropy you extend to mere strangers."

" Of course," he said. " Your wish is reasonable; and I am far from regarding you as a stranger."

This, spoken in a cool, tranquil tone, was mortifying and baffling enough. Had I attended to the suggestions of pride and ire, I should immediately have left him : but something worked within me more strongly than those feelings could. I deeply venerated my cousin's talent and principle. His friendship was of value to me : to lose it tried me severely. I would not so soon relinquish the attempt to reconquer it.

" Must we part in this way, St. John ? And when you go to India, will you leave me so, without a kinder word than you have yet spoken ?"

He now turned quite from the moon, and faced me.

"When I go to India, Jane, will I leave you? What! do you not go to India?"

"You said I could not, unless I married you."

"And you will not marry me? You adhere to that resolution?"

Reader, do you know, as I do, what terror those cold people can put into the ice of their questions? How much of the fall of the avalanche is in their anger? of the breaking up of the frozen sea in their displeasure?

"No, St. John, I will not marry you. I adhere to my resolution."

The avalanche had shaken and slid a little forward; but it did not yet crash down.

"Once more, why this refusal?" he asked.

"Formerly," I answered, "because you did not love me; now, I reply, because you almost hate me. If I were to marry you, you would kill me. You are killing me now."

His lips and cheeks turned white — quite white.

"*I should kill—I am killing you?* Your words are such as ought not to be used: violent, unfeminine, and untrue. They betray an unfortunate state of mind: they merit severe reproof: they would seem inexcusable; but that it is the duty of man to forgive his fellow, even until seventy-and-seven times."

I had finished the business now. While earnestly wishing to erase from his mind the trace of my former offence, I had stamped on that tenacious surface, another and far deeper impression : I had burnt it in.

" Now you will indeed hate me," I said. " It is useless to attempt to conciliate you : I see I have made an eternal enemy of you."

A fresh wrong did these words inflict : the worse, because they touched on the truth. That bloodless lip quivered to a temporary spasm. I knew the steely ire I had whetted. I was heart-wrung.

" You utterly misinterpret my words," I said, at once seizing his hand : " I have no intention to grieve or pain you—indeed, I have not."

Most bitterly he smiled—most decidedly he withdrew his hand from mine. " And now you recall your promise, and will not go to India at all, I presume ?" said he, after a considerable pause.

"Yes I will, as your assistant," I answered.

A very long silence succeeded. What struggle there was in him between Nature and Grace in this interval, I cannot tell: only singular gleams scintillated in his eyes, and strange shadows passed over his face. He spoke at last.

"I before proved to you the absurdity of a single woman of your age proposing to accompany abroad a single man of mine. I proved it to you in such terms as, I should have thought, would have prevented your ever again alluding to the plan. That you have done so, I regret—for your sake."

I interrupted him. Anything like a tangible reproach gave me courage at once. " Keep to common sense, St. John : you are verging on nonsense. You pretend to be shocked by what I have said. You are not really shocked; for, with your superior mind, you cannot be either so dull or so conceited as to misunderstand my meaning. I say again, I will be your curate, if you like, but never your wife."

Again he turned lividly pale; but, as before, controlled his passion perfectly. He answered emphatically, but calmly :—

" A female curate, who is not my wife, would never suit me. With me, then, it seems, you cannot go: but if you are sincere in your offer, I will, while in town, speak to a married missionary, whose wife needs a coad-

jutor.   Your own fortune will make you independent of the Society's aid; and thus you
may still be spared the dishonour of breaking
your promise, and deserting the band you
engaged to join."

Now I never had, as the reader knows,
either given any formal promise, or entered
into any engagement; and this language was
all much too hard, and much too despotic for
the occasion.   I replied :—

"There is no dishonour ; no breach of promise ; no desertion in the case.   I am not
under the slightest obligation to go to India :
especially with strangers.   With you, I would
have ventured much ; because I admire, con-
fide in, and, as a sister, I love you : but I am
convinced that, go when and with whom I
would, I should not live long in that climate."

"Ah! you are afraid of yourself," he said,
curling his lip.

"I am.   God did not give me my life to
throw away ; and to do as you wish me, would,
I begin to think, be almost equivalent to com-
mitting suicide.   Moreover, before I definitively
resolve on quitting England, I will know for
certain, whether I cannot be of greater use by
remaining in it than by leaving it."

"What do you mean ?"

"It would be fruitless to attempt to explain: but there is a point on which I have long endured painful doubt; and I can go nowhere till by some means that doubt is removed."

"I know where your heart turns, and to what it clings. The interest you cherish is lawless and unconsecrated. Long since you ought to have crushed it: now you should blush to allude to it. You think of Mr. Rochester?"

It was true. I confessed it by silence.

"Are you going to seek Mr. Rochester?"

"I must find out what is become of him."

"It remains for me, then," he said, "to remember you in my prayers; and to entreat God for you, in all earnestness, that you may not indeed become a castaway. I had thought I recognised in you one of the chosen. But God sees not as man sees: *His* will be done."

He opened the gate, passed through it, and strayed away down the glen. He was soon out of sight.

On re-entering the parlour, I found Diana standing at the window, looking very thoughtful. Diana was a great deal taller than I: she put her hand on my shoulder, and, stooping, examined my face.

"Jane," she said, "you are always agitated and pale now. I am sure there is something the matter. Tell me what business St. John and you have on hands. I have watched you this half hour from the window: you must forgive my being such a spy, but for a long time I have fancied I hardly know what. St. John is a strange being ——"

She paused—I did not speak: soon she resumed:—

"That brother of mine cherishes peculiar views of some sort respecting you, I am sure: he has long distinguished you by a notice and interest he never showed any one else—to what end? I wish he loved you—does he, Jane?"

I put her cool hand to my hot forehead: "No, Die, not one whit."

"Then why does he follow you so with his eyes—and get you so frequently alone with him, and keep you so continually at his side? Mary and I had both concluded he wished you to marry him."

"He does—he has asked me to be his wife."

Diana clapped her hands. "That is just what we hoped and thought! And you will marry him, Jane, won't you? And then he will stay in England."

"Far from that Diana; his sole idea in proposing to me is to procure a fitting fellow-
labourer in his Indian toils."

"What! He wishes you to go to India?"

"Yes."

"Madness!" she exclaimed. "You would
not live three months there, I am certain. You
never shall go: you have not consented—have
you, Jane?"

"I have refused to marry him ——."

"And have consequently displeased him?"
she suggested.

"Deeply: he will never forgive me, I fear:
yet I offered to accompany him as his sister."

"It was frantic folly to do so, Jane. Think
of the task you undertook—one of incessant
fatigue: where fatigue kills even the strong;
and you are weak. St. John—you know him
—would urge you to impossibilities: with him
there would be no permission to rest during
the hot hours; and unfortunately, I have noticed, whatever he exacts, you force yourself
to perform. I am astonished you found courage
to refuse his hand. You do not love him then,
Jane?"

"Not as a husband."

"Yet he is a handsome fellow."

"And I am so plain you see, Die. We should never suit."

"Plain! You? Not at all. You are much too pretty, as well as too good, to be grilled alive in Calcutta." And again she earnestly conjured me to give up all thoughts of going out with her brother.

"I must, indeed," I said; "for when just now I repeated the offer of serving him for a deacon, he expressed himself shocked at my want of decency. He seemed to think I had committed an impropriety in proposing to accompany him unmarried: as if I had not from the first hoped to find in him a brother; and habitually regarded him as such."

"What makes you say he does not love you, Jane?"

"You should hear himself on the subject. He has again and again explained that it is not himself, but his office he wishes to mate. He has told me I am formed for labour—not for love: which is true, no doubt. But, in my opinion, if I am not formed for love, it follows that I am not formed for marriage. Would it not be strange, Die, to be chained for life to a man who regarded one but as a useful tool?"

" Insupportable — unnatural — out of the question !"

" And then," I continued; " though I have only sisterly affection for him now, yet, if forced to be his wife, I can imagine the possibility of conceiving an inevitable, strange, torturing kind of love for him : because he is so talented ; and there is often a certain heroic grandeur in his look, manner, and conversation. In that case, my lot would become unspeakably wretched. He would not want me to love him ; and if I showed the feeling, he would make me sensible that it was a superfluity, unrequired by him, unbecoming in me. I know he would."

" And yet, St. John is a good man," said Diana.

" He is a good and a great man : but he forgets, pitilessly, the feelings and claims of little people, in pursuing his own large views. It is better, therefore, for the insignificant to keep out of his way; lest, in his progress, he should trample them down. Here he comes ! I will leave you, Diana." And I hastened up stairs, as I saw him entering the garden.

But I was forced to meet him again at supper. During that meal he appeared just as composed as usual. I had thought he would hardly speak to me, and I was certain he had given up the pursuit of his matrimonial scheme : the sequel showed I was mistaken on both points. He addressed me precisely in his ordinary manner; or what had, of late, been his ordinary manner : one scrupulously polite. No doubt he had invoked the help of the Holy Spirit to subdue the anger I had roused in him, and now believed he had forgiven me once more.

For the evening reading before prayers, he selected the twenty-first chapter of Revelations. It was at all times pleasant to listen, while from his lips fell the words of the Bible : never did his fine voice sound at once so sweet and full— never did his manner become so impressive in its noble simplicity, as when he delivered the oracles of God ; and to-night that voice took a more solemn tone—that manner a more thrilling meaning—as he sat in the midst of his household circle (the May moon shining in through the uncurtained window, and rendering almost unnecessary the light of the candle on the table) : as he sat there, bending over the great old Bible, and described from its page the vision of the new heaven and the new earth— told how God would come to dwell with men, how he would wipe away all tears from their eyes, and promised that there should be no more death, neither sorrow nor crying, nor any more pain, because the former things were passed away.

The succeeding words thrilled me strangely as he spoke them: especially as I felt, by the slight, indescribable alteration in sound, that in uttering them, his eye had turned on me.

"He that overcometh shall inherit all things; and I will be his God, and he shall be my son. But," was slowly, distinctly read, "the fearful, the unbelieving, &c., shall have their part in the lake which burneth with fire and brimstone, which is the second death."

Henceforward, I knew what fate St. John feared for me.

A calm, subdued triumph, blent with a longing earnestness, marked his enunciation of the last glorious verses of that chapter. The reader believed his name was already written in the Lamb's book of life, and he yearned after the hour which should admit him to the city to which the kings of the earth bring their glory and honour; which has no need of sun or moon to shine in it, because the glory of God lightens it, and the Lamb is the light thereof.

In the prayer following the chapter, all his

energy gathered—all his stern zeal woke : he was in deep earnest, wrestling with God, and resolved on a conquest. He supplicated strength for the weak-hearted; guidance for wanderers from the fold : a return, even at the eleventh hour, for those whom the temptations of the world and the flesh were luring from the narrow path. He asked, he urged, he claimed the boon of a brand snatched from the burning. Earnestness is ever deeply solemn : first, as I listened to that prayer, I wondered at his ; then, when it continued and rose, I was touched by it, and at last awed. He felt the greatness and goodness of his purpose so sincerely : others who heard him plead for it, could not but feel it too.

The prayer over, we took leave of him : he was to go at a very early hour in the morning. Diana and Mary having kissed him, left the room—in compliance, I think, with a whispered hint from him : I tendered my hand, and wished him a pleasant journey.

" Thank you, Jane. As I said, I shall return from Cambridge in a fortnight : that space, then, is yet left you for reflection. If I listened to human pride, I should say no more to you of marriage with me ; but I listen to my duty, and keep steadily in view my first aim—to do all things to the glory of God. My Master was long-suffering: so will I be. I cannot give you up to perdition as a vessel of wrath: repent —resolve; while there is yet time. Remember, we are bid to work while it is day—warned that " the night cometh when no man shall work." Remember the fate of Dives, who had his good things in this life. God give you strength to choose that better part which shall not be taken from you!"

He laid his hand on my head as he uttered the last words. He had spoken earnestly, mildly: his look was not, indeed, that of a lover beholding his mistress; but it was that of a pastor recalling his wandering sheep—or better, of a guardian angel watching the soul for which he is responsible. All men of talent, whether they be men of feeling or not; whether they be zealots, or aspirants, or despots—provided only they be sincere—have their sublime moments: when they subdue and rule. I felt veneration for St. John—veneration so strong that its impetus thrust me at once to the point I had so long shunned. I was tempted to cease struggling with him—to rush down the torrent of his will into the gulf of his existence, and there lose my own. I was almost as hard beset by him now as I had been once before, in a different way, by another. I was a fool both times. To have yielded then would have been an error of principle; to have yielded now would have been an error of judgment. So I think at this hour, when I look back to the crisis through the quiet medium of time: I was unconscious of folly at the instant.

I stood motionless under my hierophant's touch. My refusals were forgotten—my fears overcome—my wrestlings paralyzed. The Impossible—*i. e.* my marriage with St. John—was fast becoming the Possible. All was changing utterly, with a sudden sweep. Religion called—Angels beckoned—God commanded—life rolled together like a scroll—death's gates opening, shewed eternity beyond: it seemed, that for safety and bliss there, all here might be sacrificed in a second. The dim room was full of visions.

" Could you decide now?" asked the missionary. The inquiry was put in gentle tones: he drew me to him as gently. Oh, that gentleness! how far more potent is it than force! I could resist St. John's wrath: I grew pliant as a reed under his kindness. Yet I knew all the time, if I yielded now, I should not the less be made to repent, some day, of my former rebel-

lion. His nature was not changed by one hour
of solemn prayer: it was only elevated.

"I could decide if I were but certain," I
answered: "were I but convinced that it is
God's will I should marry you, I could vow to
marry you here and now—come afterwards
what would!"

"My prayers are heard!" ejaculated St.
John. He pressed his hand firmer on my head,
as if he claimed me: he surrounded me with
his arm, *almost* as if he loved me (I say *almost*
—I knew the difference—for I had felt what it
was to be loved; but, like him, I had now put
love out of the question, and thought only of
duty): I contended with my inward dimness
of vision, before which clouds yet rolled. I
sincerely, deeply, fervently longed to do what
was right; and only that. "Shew me—shew
me the path!" I entreated of Heaven. I was
excited more than I had ever been; and whether
what followed was the effect of excitement, the
reader shall judge.

All the house was still; for I believe all, except St. John and myself, were now retired to
rest. The one candle was dying out: the room
was full of moonlight. My heart beat fast and
thick: I heard its throb. Suddenly it stood
still to an inexpressible feeling that thrilled it

through, and passed at once to my head and extremities. The feeling was not like an electric shock; but it was quite as sharp, as strange, as startling: it acted on my senses as if their utmost activity hitherto had been but torpor; from which they were now summoned, and forced to wake. They rose expectant: eye and ear waited, while the flesh quivered on my bones.

"What have you heard? What do you see?" asked St. John. I saw nothing: but I heard a voice somewhere cry—

"Jane! Jane! Jane!" Nothing more.

"Oh, God! what is it?" I gasped.

I might have said, "Where is it?" for it did not seem in the room—nor in the house—nor in the garden: it did not come out of the air— nor from under the earth—nor from overhead. I had heard it—where, or whence, for ever impossible to know! And it was the voice of a human being—a known, loved, well-remembered voice—that of Edward Fairfax Rochester; and it spoke in pain and woe—wildly, eerily, urgently.

"I am coming!" I cried. "Wait for me! Oh, I will come!" I flew to the door, and looked into the passage: it was dark. I ran out into the garden: it was void.

"Where are you?" I exclaimed.

The hills beyond Marsh-Glen sent the answer faintly back—"Where are you!" I listened. The wind sighed low in the firs: all was moorland loneliness and midnight hush.

"Down superstition!" I commented, as that spectre rose up black by the black yew at the gate. "This is not thy deception, nor thy witchcraft: it is the work of nature. She was roused, and did—no miracle—but her best."

I broke from St. John; who had followed, and would have detained me. It was *my* turn to assume ascendancy. *My* powers were in play, and in force. I told him to forbear question or remark; I desired him to leave me: I must, and would be alone. He obeyed at once. Where there is energy to command well enough, obedience never fails. I mounted to my chamber; locked myself in; fell on my knees; and prayed in my way—a different way to St. John's, but effective in its own fashion. I seemed to penetrate very near a Mighty Spirit; and my soul rushed out in gratitude at His feet. I rose from the thanksgiving—took a resolve—and lay down, unscared, enlightened—eager but for the daylight.

CHAPTER X.

THE daylight came. I rose at dawn. I busied
myself for an hour or two with arranging my
things in my chamber, drawers and wardrobe,
in the order wherein I should wish to leave them
during a brief absence. Meantime, I heard St.
John quit his room. He stopped at my door:
I feared he would knock—no, but a slip of
paper was passed under the door. I took it up.
It bore these words:—

"You left me too suddenly last night. Had
you stayed but a little longer, you would have
laid your hand on the Christian's cross and
the angel's crown. I shall expect your clear
decision when I return this day fortnight.
Meantime, watch and pray that you enter not
into temptation: the spirit, I trust, is willing,
but the flesh, I see, is weak. I shall pray for
you hourly.—Yours, St. John."

"My spirit," I answered mentally, "is willing

to do what is right; and my flesh, I hope, is strong enough to accomplish the will of Heaven, when once that will is distinctly known to me. At any rate, it shall be strong enough to search—inquire—to grope an outlet from this cloud of doubt, and find the open day of certainty."

It was the first of June; yet the morning was overcast and chilly: rain beat fast on my casement. I heard the front-door open, and St. John pass out. Looking through the window, I saw him traverse the garden. He took the way over the misty moors in the direction of Whitcross—there he would meet the coach.

"In a few more hours I shall succeed you in that track, cousin," thought I: "I too have a coach to meet at Whitcross. I too have some to see and ask after in England, before I depart for ever."

It wanted yet two hours of breakfast-time. I filled the interval in walking softly about my room, and pondering the visitation which had given my plans their present bent. I recalled that inward sensation I had experienced : for I could recall it, with all its unspeakable strangeness. I recalled the voice I had heard; again I questioned whence it came, as vainly as before : it seemed in *me*—not in the external world. I asked, was it a mere nervous impression—a delusion? I could not conceive or believe it: it was more like an inspiration. The wondrous shock of feeling had come like the earthquake which shook the foundations of Paul and Silas's prison: it had opened the doors of the soul's cell, and loosed its bands—it had wakened it out of its sleep, whence it sprang trembling, listening, aghast; then vibrated thrice a cry on my startled ear, and in my quaking heart, and through my spirit; which neither feared nor shook, but exulted as if in joy over the success of one effort it had been privileged to make, independent of the cumbrous body.

"Ere many days," I said, as I terminated my musings, "I will know something of him whose voice seemed last night to summon me. Letters have proved of no avail—personal inquiry shall replace them."

At breakfast, I announced to Diana and Mary that I was going a journey, and should be absent at least four days.

"Alone, Jane?" they asked.

"Yes; it was to see, or hear news of, a friend about whom I had for some time been uneasy."

They might have said, as I have no doubt they thought, that they had believed me to be without any friends save them: for, indeed, I had often said so; but with their true, natural delicacy, they abstained from comment: except that Diana asked me if I was sure I was well enough to travel. I looked very pale, she observed. I replied that nothing ailed me save anxiety of mind, which I hoped soon to alleviate.

It was easy to make my further arrangements; for I was troubled with no inquiries—no surmises. Having once explained to them that I could not now be explicit about my plans, they kindly and wisely acquiesced in the silence with which I pursued them; according to me the privilege of free action I should, under similar circumstances, have accorded them.

I left Moor-House at three o'clock, P.M., and soon after four, I stood at the foot of the signpost of Whitcross, waiting the arrival of the coach which was to take me to distant Thornfield. Amidst the silence of those solitary roads and desert hills, I heard it approach from a great distance. It was the same vehicle whence, a year ago, I had alighted one summer evening on this very spot—how desolate, and hopeless, and objectless! It stopped as I beckoned. I entered—not now obliged to part with my whole fortune as the price of its accommodation. Once more on the road to Thornfield, I felt like the messenger-pigeon flying home.

It was a journey of six-and-thirty hours. I had set out from Whitcross on a Tuesday afternoon, and early on the succeeding Thursday morning the coach stopped to water the horses at a wayside inn, situated in the midst of scenery whose green hedges and large fields, and low, pastoral hills (how mild of feature and verdant of hue compared with the stern north-midland moors of Morton!) met my eye like the lineaments of a once familiar face. Yes, I knew the character of this landscape: I was sure we were near my bourne.

"How far is Thornfield-Hall from here?" I asked of the ostler.

"Just two miles, ma'am, across the fields."

"My journey is closed," I thought to myself. I got out of the coach, gave a box I had into the ostler's charge, to be kept till I called for it; paid my fare; satisfied the coachman, and was going: the brightening day gleamed on the sign of the inn, and I read in gilt letters "The Rochester Arms." My heart leapt up: I was already on my master's very lands. It fell again: the thought struck it:—

"Your master himself may be beyond the British Channel, for aught you know: and then, if he is at Thornfield-Hall, towards which you hasten, who besides him is there? His lunatic wife; and you have nothing to do with him: you dare not speak to him or seek his presence. You have lost your labour—you had better go no farther," urged the monitor. "Ask information of the people at the inn; they can give you all you seek : they can solve your doubts at once. Go up to that man, and inquire if Mr. Rochester be at home."

The suggestion was sensible; and yet I could not force myself to act on it. I so dreaded a reply that would crush me with despair. To prolong doubt was to prolong hope. I might yet once more see the Hall under the ray of her star. There was the stile before me—the very fields through which I had hurried, blind, deaf, distracted, with a revengeful fury tracking and scourging me, on the morning I fled from Thornfield: ere I well knew what course I had resolved to take, I was in the midst of them. How fast I walked! How I ran sometimes! How I looked forward to catch the first view of the well-known woods! With what feelings I welcomed single trees I knew, and familiar glimpses of meadow and hill between them!

At last the woods rose; the rookery clustered dark; a loud cawing broke the morning stillness.

Strange delight inspired me: on I hastened. Another field crossed—a lane threaded—and there were the court-yard walls—the back-offices: the house itself, the rookery still hid.

"My first view of it shall be in front," I determined, "where its bold battlements will strike the eye nobly at once, and where I can single out my master's very window: perhaps he will be standing at it—he rises early: perhaps he is now walking in the orchard, or on the pavement in front. Could I but see him! —but a moment! Surely, in that case, I should not be so mad as to run to him? I cannot tell —I am not certain. And if I did—what then? God bless him! What then? Who would be hurt by my once more tasting the life his glance can give me?—I rave: perhaps at this moment he is watching the sun rise over the Pyrenees, or on the tideless sea of the south."

I had coasted along the lower wall of the orchard—turned its angle: there was a gate just there, opening into the meadow, between two stone pillars, crowned by stone balls. From behind one pillar, I could peep round quietly at the full front of the mansion. I advanced my head with precaution, desirous to ascertain if any bedroom window-blinds were yet drawn up: battlements, windows, long front—all from this sheltered station were at my command.

The crows sailing overhead perhaps watched me while I took this survey. I wonder what they thought: they must have considered I was very careful and timid at first, and that gradually I grew very bold and reckless. A peep, and then a long stare; and then a departure from my niche and a straying out into the meadow; and a sudden stop full in front of the great mansion, and a protracted, hardy gaze towards it. "What affectation of diffidence was this at first!" they might have demanded, "What stupid regardlessness now?"

Hear an illustration, reader.

A lover finds his mistress asleep on a mossy bank; he wishes to catch a glimpse of her fair face without waking her. He steals softly over the grass, careful to make no sound; he pauses—fancying she has stirred: he withdraws; not for worlds would he be seen. All is still: he again advances: he bends above her; a light veil rests on her features: he lifts it, bends lower; now his eyes anticipate the vision of beauty—warm and blooming and lovely in rest. How hurried was their first glance! But how they fix! How he starts! How he suddenly and vehemently clasps in both arms the form he dared not, a moment since, touch with his finger! How he calls aloud a name, and drops his burden, and gazes on it wildly! He thus grasps and cries, and gazes, because he no longer fears to waken by any sound he can utter—by any movement he can make. He thought his love slept sweetly: he finds she is stone-dead.

I looked with timorous joy towards a stately house: I saw a blackened ruin.

No need to cower behind a gate-post, indeed! —to peep up at chamber lattices, fearing life was astir behind them! No need to listen for doors opening—to fancy steps on the pavement or the gravel-walk! The lawn, the grounds were trodden and waste: the portal yawned void. The front was, as I had once seen it in a dream, but a shell-like wall, very high and very fragile looking, perforated with paneless windows: no roof, no battlements, no chimneys—all had crashed in.

And there was the silence of death about it: the solitude of a lonesome wild. No wonder that letters addressed to people here had never received an answer: as well despatch epistles to a vault in a church-aisle. The grim blackness of the stones told by what fate the Hall had fallen—by conflagration: but how kindled? What story belonged to this disaster? What loss, besides mortar, and marble, and wood-work, had followed upon it? Had life been wrecked, as well as property? If so, whose? Dreadful question: there was no one here to answer it—not even dumb sign, mute token.

In wandering round the shattered walls and through the devastated interior, I gathered evidence that the calamity was not of late occurrence. Winter snows, I thought, had drifted through that void arch, winter rains beaten in at those hollow casements; for, amidst the drenched piles of rubbish, spring had cherished vegetation: grass and weed grew here and there between the stones and fallen rafters. And, oh! where, meantime, was the hapless owner of this wreck? In what land? Under what auspices? My eye involuntarily wandered to the grey church tower near the gates, and I asked, "Is he with Damer de Rochester, sharing the shelter of his narrow marble house?"

Some answer must be had to these ques-tions. I could find it nowhere but at the inn; and thither, ere long, I returned. The host himself brought my breakfast into the parlour. I requested him to shut the door and sit down : I had some questions to ask him. But when he complied, I scarcely knew how to begin ; such horror had I of the possible answers. And yet the spectacle of desolation I had just left, prepared me in a measure for a tale of misery. The host was a respectable-looking, middle-aged man.

"You know Thornfield Hall, of course ?" I managed to say at last.

"Yes, ma'am ; I lived there once."

"Did you ?" Not in my time, I thought : you are a stranger to me.

"I was the late Mr. Rochester's butler," he added.

The late ! I seemed to have received with full force the blow I had been trying to evade.

"The late !" I gasped. "Is he dead ?"

"I mean the present gentleman, Mr. Edward's father," he explained. I breathed again : my blood resumed its flow. Fully assured by these words that Mr. Edward—*my* Mr. Rochester (God bless him, wherever he was !)—was at least alive : was, in short, "the present gentleman," (gladdening words !) it seemed I could hear all that was to come—whatever the disclosures might be—with comparative tranquillity. Since he was not in the grave, I could bear, I thought, to learn that he was at the Antipodes.

"Is Mr. Rochester living at Thornfield Hall now?" I asked: knowing, of course, what the answer would be, but yet desirous of deferring the direct question as to where he really was.

"No, ma'am—oh, no! No one is living there. I suppose you are a stranger in these parts, or you would have heard what happened last autumn. Thornfield Hall is quite a ruin: it was burnt down just about harvest time—A dreadful calamity! such an immense quantity of valuable property destroyed: hardly any of the furniture could be saved. The fire broke out at dead of night, and before the engines arrived from Millcote, the building was one mass of flame. It was a terrible spectacle: I witnessed it myself."

"At dead of night!" I muttered. Yes, that was ever the hour of fatality at Thornfield. "Was it known how it originated?" I demanded.

"They guessed, ma'am: they guessed. Indeed, I should say it was ascertained beyond a doubt. You are not perhaps aware," he continued, edging his chair a little nearer the

table, and speaking low, " that there was lady,
—a—a lunatic, kept in the house?"

" I have heard something of it."

" She was kept in very close confinement,
ma'am: people even for some years was not
absolutely certain of her existence. No one
saw her: they only knew by rumour that such
a person was at the Hall; and who or what
she was it was difficult to conjecture. They
said Mr. Edward had brought her from
abroad; and some believed she had been his
mistress. But a queer thing happened a year
since—a very queer thing."

I feared now to hear my own story. I
endeavoured to recall him to the main fact.

" And this lady?"

" This lady, ma'am," he answered, " turned
out to be Mr. Rochester's wife! The discovery was brought about in the strangest way.
There was a young lady, a governess at the
Hall, that Mr. Rochester fell in—"

" But the fire?" I suggested.

" I'm coming to that, ma'am—that Mr.
Edward fell in love with. The servants say
they never saw anybody so much in love as
he was: he was after her continually. They
used to watch him—servants will, you know,
ma'am—and he set store on her past every-

thing : for all, nobody but him thought her so very handsome. She was a little small thing, they say, almost like a child. I never saw her myself; but I've heard Leah, the housemaid, tell of her. Leah liked her well enough. Mr. Rochester was about forty, and this governess not twenty; and, you see, when gentlemen of his age fall in love with girls, they are often like as if they were bewitched : well, he would marry her."

"You shall tell me this part of the story another time," I said; but now I have a particular reason for wishing to hear all about the fire. Was it suspected that this lunatic, Mrs. Rochester, had any hand in it?"

"You've hit it, ma'am : it's quite certain that it was her, and nobody but her, that set it going. She had a woman to take care of her called Mrs. Poole—an able woman in her line, and very trustworthy; but for one fault —a fault common to a deal of them nurses and matrons—*she kept a private bottle of gin by her*, and now and then took a drop over much. It's excusable, for she had a hard life of it : but still it was dangerous; for, when Mrs. Poole was fast asleep, after the gin and water, the mad lady, who was as cunning as a witch, would take the keys out of her pocket, let herself out of her chamber, and go roaming about the house, doing any wild mischief that came into her head. They say she had nearly burnt her husband in his bed once : but I don't know about that. However, on this night, she set fire first to the hangings of the room next her own ; and then she got down to a lower story, and made her way to the chamber that had been the governess's—(she was like as if she knew somehow how matters had gone on, and had a spite at her)—and she kindled the bed there : but there was nobody sleeping in it, fortunately. The governess had run away two months before ; and for all Mr. Rochester sought her as if she had been the most precious thing he had in the world, he could never hear a word of her ; and he grew savage—quite savage on his disappointment : he never was a wild man, but he got dangerous after he lost her. He would be alone, too. He sent Mrs. Fairfax, the housekeeper, away to her friends at a distance ; but he did it handsomely, for he settled an annuity on her for life : and she deserved it—she was a very good woman. Miss Adèle, a ward he had, was put to school. He broke off acquaintance with all the gentry, and shut himself up, like a hermit, at the Hall."

"What! did he not leave England?"

"Leave England? Bless you, no! He would not cross the door-stones of the house; except at night, when he walked just like a ghost about the grounds and in the orchard as if he had lost his senses—which it is my opinion he had; for a more spirited, bolder, keener gentleman than he was before that midge of a governess crossed him, you never saw, ma'am. He was not a man given to wine, or cards, or racing, as some are, and he was not so very handsome; but he had a courage and a will of his own, if ever man had. I knew him from a boy, you see: and for my part I have often wished that Miss Eyre had been sunk in the sea before she came to Thornfield Hall."

"Then Mr. Rochester was at home when the fire broke out?"

"Yes, indeed was he; and he went up to the attics when all was burning above and below, and got the servants out of their beds and helped them down himself—and went back to get his mad wife out of her cell. And then they called out to him that she was on the roof; where she was standing, waving her arms, above the battlements, and shouting out till they could hear her a mile off: I saw her and heard her with my own eyes. She was a big woman, and had long, black hair: we could see it streaming against the flames as she stood. I witnessed, and several more witnessed Mr. Rochester ascend through the skylight on to the roof: we heard him call "Bertha!" We saw him approach her; and then, ma'am, she yelled, and gave a spring, and the next minute she lay smashed on the pavement."

" Dead?"

" Dead? Aye, dead as the stones on which her brains and blood were scattered."

"Good God!"

" You may well say so, ma'am: it was frightful!"

He shuddered.

" And afterwards?" I urged.

" Well, ma'am, afterwards the house was burnt to the ground: there are only some bits of walls standing now."

" Were any other lives lost?"

" No—perhaps it would have been better if there had."

" What do you mean?"

" Poor Mr. Edward!" he ejaculated, " I little thought ever to have seen it! Some say it was a just judgment on him for keeping his first marriage secret, and wanting to take another wife while he had one living : but I pity him, for my part."

"You said he was alive?" I exclaimed.

"Yes, yes : he is alive; but many think he had better be dead."

"Why? How?" My blood was again running cold.

"Where is he?" I demanded. "Is he in England?"

"Aye—aye—he's in England; he can't get out of England, I fancy—he's a fixture now."

What agony was this? And the man seemed resolved to protract it !

"He is stone-blind," he said at last. "Yes —he is stone-blind—is Mr. Edward."

I had dreaded worse. I had dreaded he was mad. I summoned strength to ask what had caused this calamity.

"It was all his own courage, and a body may say, his kindness, in a way, ma'am : he wouldn't leave the house till every one else was out before him. As he came down the great stair-case at last, after Mrs. Rochester had flung herself from the battlements, there was a great crash—all fell. He was taken out from under the ruins, alive, but sadly hurt : a beam had fallen in such a way as to protect him partly; but one eye was knocked out, and one hand so crushed that Mr. Carter, the surgeon, had to amputate it directly. The other eye inflamed: he lost the sight of that also. He is now helpless, indeed—blind and a cripple."

"Where is he? Where does he now live?"

"At Ferndean, a manor-house on a farm he has, about thirty miles off: quite a desolate spot."

"Who is with him?"

"Old John and his wife: he would have none else. He is quite broken down, they say."

"Have you any sort of conveyance?"

"We have a chaise, ma'am, a very handsome chaise."

"Let it be got ready instantly; and if your post-boy can drive me to Ferndean before dark this day, I'll pay both you and him twice the hire you usually demand."

CHAPTER XI.

THE manor-house of Ferndean was a building
of considerable antiquity, moderate size, and
no architectural pretensions, deep buried in a
wood. I had heard of it before. Mr. Rochester often spoke of it, and sometimes went
there. His father had purchased the estate for
the sake of the game covers. He would have
let the house; but could find no tenant, in consequence of its ineligible and insalubrious site.
Ferndean then remained uninhabited and un-
furnished; with the exception of some two or
three rooms fitted up for the accommodation
of the squire when he went there in the season
to shoot.

To this house I came, just ere dark, on an
evening marked by the characteristics of sad
sky, cold gale, and continued small, penetrating rain. The last mile I performed on foot,
having dismissed the chaise and driver with

the double remuneration I had promised.
Even when within a very short distance of the
manor-house, you could see nothing of it; so
thick and dark grew the timber of the gloomy
wood about it.   Iron gates between granite
pillars showed me where to enter, and passing
through them, I found myself at once in the
twilight of close-ranked trees.   There was a
grass-grown track descending the forest-aisle,
between hoar and knotty shafts and under
branched arches. I followed it, expecting soon
to reach the dwelling ; but it stretched on and
on, it wound far and farther : no sign of habitation or grounds was visible.

I thought I had taken a wrong direction
and lost my way.   The darkness of natural as
well as of sylvan dusk, gathered over me : I
looked round in search of another road.   There
was none : all was interwoven stem, columnar
trunk, dense, summer foliage — no opening
anywhere.

I proceeded : at last my way opened, the
trees thinned a little ; presently I beheld a rail-
ing, then the house—scarce, by this dim light,
distinguishable from the trees ; so dank and
green were its decaying walls.   Entering a
portal, fastened only by a latch, I stood amidst
a space of enclosed ground, from which the

wood swept away in a semicircle. There were no flowers, no garden-beds; only a broad gravel-walk girdling a grass-plat, and this set in the heavy frame of the forest. The house presented two pointed gables in its front; the windows were latticed and narrow: the front-door was narrow too, one step led up to it. The whole looked, as the host of the Rochester Arms had said, "quite a desolate spot." It was as still as a church on a week-day: the pattering rain on the forest leaves was the only sound audible in its vicinage.

"Can there be life here?" I asked.

Yes: life of some kind there was; for I heard a movement—that narrow front-door was unclosing, and some shape was about to issue from the grange.

It opened slowly: a figure came out into the twilight and stood on the step; a man without a hat: he stretched forth his hand as if to feel whether it rained. Dusk as it was, I had recognised him;—it was my master, Edward Fairfax Rochester, and no other.

I stayed my step, almost my breath, and stood to watch him—to examine him, myself unseen, and alas! to him invisible. It was a sudden meeting, and one in which rapture was kept well in check by pain. I had no

difficulty in restraining my voice from exclamation, my step from hasty advance.

His form was of the same strong and stal-
wart contour as ever : his port was still erect,
his hair was still raven-black ; nor were his
features altered or sunk : not in one year's
space, by any sorrow, could his athletic
strength be quelled, or his vigorous prime
blighted.   But in his countenance, I saw a
change : that looked desperate and brooding—
that reminded me of some wronged and fettered wild-beast or bird, dangerous to approach
in his sullen woe.   The caged eagle, whose
gold-ringed eyes cruelty has extinguished,
might look as looked that sightless Samson.

And, reader, do you think I feared him in
his blind ferocity?—if you do, you little know
me.   A soft hope blent with my sorrow that
soon I should dare to drop a kiss on that brow
of rock, and on those lids so sternly sealed
beneath it : but not yet.   I would not accost
him yet.

He descended the one step, and advanced
slowly and gropingly towards the grass plat.
Where was his daring stride now ?   Then he
paused, as if he knew not which way to turn.
He lifted his hand and opened his eyelids ;
gazed blank, and with a straining effort, on

the sky, and towards the amphitheatre of trees: one saw that all to him was void darkness. He stretched his right hand (the left arm, the mutilated one, he kept hidden in his bosom); he seemed to wish by touch to gain an idea of what lay round him: he met but vacancy still; for the trees were some yards off where he stood. He relinquished the endeavour, folded his arms, and stood quiet and mute in the rain, now falling fast on his uncovered head. At this moment John approached from some quarter.

"Will you take my arm, sir?" he said; "there is a heavy shower coming on: had you not better go in?"

"Let me alone," was the answer.

John withdrew, without having observed me. Mr. Rochester now tried to walk about: vainly,—all was too uncertain. He groped his way back to the house, and, re-entering it, closed the door.

I now drew near and knocked: John's wife opened for me. "Mary," I said, "how are you?"

She started as if she had seen a ghost: I calmed her. To her hurried "Is it really you, Miss, come at this late hour to this 'only place?" I answered by taking her hand; and

then I followed her into the kitchen, where
John now sat by a good fire. I explained
to them, in few words, that I had heard
all which had happened since I left Thornfield, and that I was come to see Mr.
Rochester. I asked John to go down to the
turnpike-house, where I had dismissed the
chaise, and bring my trunk, which I had left
there; and then, while I removed my bonnet
and shawl, I questioned Mary as to whether I
could be accommodated at the Manor House
for the night; and finding that arrangements
to that effect, though difficult, would not be
impossible, I informed her I should stay. Just
at this moment the parlour-bell rang.

"When you go in," said I, "tell your master
that a person wishes to speak to him: but
do not give my name."

"I don't think he will see you," she answered; "he refuses everybody."

When she returned, I inquired what he had
said.

"You are to send in your name and your
business," she replied. She then proceeded to
fill a glass with water, and place it on a tray,
together with candles.

"Is that what he rang for?" I asked.

"Yes: he always has candles brought in at dark, though he is blind."

"Give the tray to me : I will carry it in."

I took it from her hand: she pointed me out the parlour door. The tray shook as I held it; the water spilt from the glass; my heart struck my ribs loud and fast. Mary opened the door for me, and shut it behind me.

This parlour looked gloomy: a neglected handful of fire burnt low in the grate; and, leaning over it, with his head supported against the high, old-fashioned mantel-piece, appeared the blind tenant of the room. His old dog, Pilot, lay on one side, removed out of the way, and coiled up as if afraid of being inadvertently trodden on. Pilot pricked up his ears when I came in; then he jumped up with a yelp and a whine, and bounded towards me: he almost knocked the tray from my hands. I set it on the table; then patted him, and said softly, "Lie down!" Mr. Rochester turned mechanically to *see* what the commotion was: but as he *saw* nothing, he returned and sighed.

"Give me the water, Mary," he said.

I approached him with the now only half-filled glass: Pilot followed me, still excited.

"What is the matter?" he inquired.

"Down, Pilot!" I again said. He checked

the water on its way to his lips, and seemed to listen : he drank, and put the glass down. "This is you, Mary, is it not?"

"Mary is in the kitchen," I answered.

He put out his hand with a quick gesture, but not seeing where I stood, he did not touch me. "Who is this? Who is this?" he demanded, trying, as it seemed, to *see* with those sightless eyes,—unavailing and distressing attempt! "Answer me—speak again!" he ordered, imperiously and aloud.

"Will you have a little more water, sir? I spilt half of what was in the glass," I said.

"*Who* is it? *What* is it? Who speaks?"

"Pilot knows me, and John and Mary know I am here : I came only this evening," I answered.

"Great God!—what delusion has come over me? What sweet madness has seized me?"

"No delusion—no madness : your mind, sir, is too strong for delusion—your health too sound for frenzy."

"And where is this speaker? Is it only a voice? Oh! I *cannot* see, but I must feel, or my heart will stop and my brain burst. Whatever—whoever you are—be perceptible to the touch or I cannot live!"

He groped : I arrested his wandering hand, and prisoned it in both mine.

"Her very fingers!" he cried; "her small, slight fingers! If so, there must be more of her."

The muscular hand broke from my custody; my arm was seized, my shoulder—neck—waist—I was entwined and gathered to him.

"Is it Jane? *What* is it? This is her shape—this is her size ——"

"And this her voice," I added. "She is all here: her heart, too. God bless you, sir! I am glad to be so near you again.'

"Jane Eyre!—Jane Eyre!" was all he said.

"My dear master," I answered, "I am Jane Eyre: I have found you out—I am come back to you."

"In truth?—in the flesh? My living Jane?"

"You touch me, sir—you hold me, and fast enough: I am not cold like a corpse, nor vacant like air, am I?"

"My living darling! These are certainly her limbs, and these her features : but I cannot be so blest after all my misery. It is a dream: such dreams as I have had at night when I have clasped her once more to my heart, as I do now; and kissed her, as thus—and felt that she loved me, and trusted she would not leave me."

"Which I never will, sir, from this day."

"Never will, says the vision? But I always woke and found it an empty mockery; and I was desolate and abandoned—my life dark, lonely, hopeless—my soul athirst and forbidden to drink—my heart famished and never to be fed. Gentle, soft dream, nestling in my arms now, you will fly, too; as your sisters have all fled before you: but kiss me before you go—embrace me, Jane."

"There, sir—and there!"

I pressed my lips to his once brilliant and now rayless eyes—I swept his hair from his brow, and kissed that too. He suddenly seemed to rouse himself: the conviction of the reality of all this seized him.

"It is you—is it Jane? You are come back to me then?"

"I am."

"And you do not lie dead in some ditch, under some stream? And you are not a pining outcast amongst strangers?"

"No, sir; I am an independent woman now."

"Independent! What do you mean, Jane?"

"My uncle in Madeira is dead, and he left me five thousand pounds."

"Ah, this is practical—this is real!" he cried: "I should never dream that. Besides, there is that peculiar voice of hers, so animating and piquant, as well as soft: it cheers my withered heart; it puts life into it.—What, Janet! Are you an independent woman? A rich woman?"

"Quite rich, sir. If you won't let me live with you, I can build a house of my own close up to your door, and you may come and sit in my parlour when you want company of an evening."

"But as you are rich, Jane, you have now, no doubt, friends who will look after you, and not suffer you to devote yourself to a blind lameter like me?"

"I told you I am independent, sir, as well as rich: I am my own mistress."

"And you will stay with me?"

"Certainly—unless you object. I will be your neighbour, your nurse, your housekeeper. I find you lonely: I will be your companion—to read to you, to walk with you, to sit with you, to wait on you, to be eyes and hands to you. Cease to look so melancholy, my dear

Master; you shall not be left desolate, so long as I live."

He replied not: he seemed serious—abstracted: he sighed; he half-opened his lips as if to speak; he closed them again. I felt a little embarrassed. Perhaps I had been too officious in my offers of companionship and aid: perhaps I had too rashly overleaped conventionalities; and he, like St. John, saw impropriety in my inconsiderateness. I had indeed made my proposal from the idea that he wished and would ask me to be his wife: an expectation, not the less certain because unexpressed, had buoyed me up, that he would claim me at once as his own. But no hint to that effect escaping him, and his countenance becoming more overcast, I suddenly remembered that I might have been all wrong, and was perhaps playing the fool unwittingly; and I began gently to withdraw myself from his arms—but he eagerly snatched me closer.

"No—no—Jane; you must not go. No—I have touched you, heard you, felt the comfort of your presence—the sweetness of your consolation: I cannot give up these joys. I have little left in myself—I must have you. The world may laugh—may call me absurd, selfish—but it does not signify. My very soul demands you: it will be satisfied; or it will take deadly vengeance on its frame."

"Well, sir, I will stay with you: I have said so."

"Yes—but you understand one thing by staying with me; and I understand another. You, perhaps, could make up your mind to be about my hand and chair—to wait on me as a kind little nurse (for you have an affectionate heart and a generous spirit, which prompt you to make sacrifices for those you pity), and that ought to suffice for me no doubt. I suppose I should now entertain none but fatherly feelings for you: do you think so? Come—tell me."

"I will think what you like, sir: I am content to be only your nurse, if you think it better."

"But you cannot always be my nurse, Janet: you are young—you must marry one day."

"I don't care about being married."

"You should care Janet: if I were what I once was, I would try to make you care—but —a sightless block!"

He relapsed again into gloom. I, on the contrary, became more cheerful and took fresh courage: these last words gave me an insight

as to where the difficulty lay; and as it was no
difficulty with me, I felt quite relieved from
my previous embarrassment.   I resumed a
livelier vein of conversation.

"It is time some one undertook to re-
humanize you," said I, parting his thick and
long-uncut locks; " for I see you are being
metamorphosed into a lion, or something of
that sort.   You have a 'faux air' of Nebuchad-
nezzar in the fields about you, that is certain :
your hair reminds me of eagle's feathers;
whether your nails are grown like bird's claws
or not, I have not yet noticed."

"On this arm, I have neither hand nor
nails;" he said, drawing the mutilated limb
from his breast, and shewing it to me.   "It is
a mere stump—a ghastly sight!   Don't you
think so, Jane?"

"It is a pity to see it; and a pity to see
your eyes—and the scar of fire on your forehead : and the worst of it is, one is in danger
of loving you too well for all this; and making
too much of you."

"I thought you would be revolted, Jane, when
you saw my arm and my cicatrized visage."

"Did you?   Don't tell me so—lest I should
say something disparaging to your judgment.
Now, let me leave you an instant, to make a

better fire and have the hearth swept up.
Can you tell when there is a good fire?"

"Yes; with the right eye I see a glow—
a ruddy haze."

"And you see the candles?"

"Very dimly—each is a luminous cloud."

"Can you see me?"

"No, my fairy: but I am only too thankful
to hear and feel you."

"When do you take supper?"

"I never take supper."

"But you shall have some to-night. I am
hungry: so are you, I dare say, only you
forget."

Summoning Mary, I soon had the room in
more cheerful order: I prepared him, likewise,
a comfortable repast. My spirits were excited,
and with pleasure and ease I talked to him
during supper, and for a long time after.
There was no harassing restraint, no repress-
ing of glee and vivacity with him; for with
him I was at perfect ease, because I knew I
suited him: all I said or did seemed either to
console or revive him. Delightful consciousness! It brought to life and light my whole
nature: in his presence I thoroughly lived;
and he lived in mine. Blind as he was, smiles

played over his face, joy dawned on his forehead : his lineaments softened and warmed.

After supper, he began to ask me many
questions, of where I had been, what I had
been doing, how I had found him out ; but I
gave him only very partial replies : it was too
late to enter into particulars that night. Besides, I wished to touch no deep-thrilling
chord—to open no fresh well of emotion in his
heart : my sole present aim was to cheer him.
Cheered, as I have said, he was : and yet but
by fits. If a moment's silence broke the conversation, he would turn restless, touch me,
then say, " Jane."

" You are altogether a human being, Jane ?
You are certain of that ?"

" I conscientiously believe so, Mr. Rochester."

" Yet how, on this dark and doleful evening,
could you so suddenly rise on my lone hearth?
I stretched my hand to take a glass of water
from a hireling, and it was given me by you :
I asked a question, expecting John's wife to
answer me, and your voice spoke at my ear."

" Because I had come in, in Mary's stead,
with the tray."

" And there is enchantment in the very hour
I am now spending with you. Who can tell

what a dark, dreary, hopeless life I have dragged on for months past? Doing nothing, expecting nothing; merging night in day; feeling but the sensation of cold when I let the fire go out, of hunger when I forgot to eat: and then a ceaseless sorrow, and, at times, a very delirium of desire to behold my Jane again. Yes: for her restoration I longed, far more than for that of my lost sight. How can it be, that Jane is with me and says she loves me? Will she not depart as suddenly as she came? To-morrow, I fear, I shall find her no more."

A common-place, practical reply, out of the train of his own disturbed ideas, was, I was sure, the best and most re-assuring for him in this frame of mind. I passed my finger over his eyebrows, and remarked that they were scorched, and that I would apply something which should make them grow as broad and black as ever.

"Where is the use of doing me good in any way, beneficent spirit, when, at some fatal moment, you will again desert me—passing like a shadow, whither and how, to me unknown; and for me, remaining afterwards undiscoverable?"

"Have you a pocket-comb about you, sir?"

"What for, Jane?"

"Just to comb out this shaggy black mane. I find you rather alarming, when I examine you close at hand: you talk of my being a fairy; but, I am sure, you are more like a brownie."

"Am I hideous, Jane?"

"Very, sir: you always were, you know."

"Humph! The wickedness has not been taken out of you, wherever you have so-journed."

"Yet I have been with good people; far better than you: a hundred times better; people possessed of ideas and views you never entertained in your life: quite more refined and exalted.'

"Who the deuce have you been with?"

"If you twist in that way, you will make me pull the hair out of your head; and then I think you will cease to entertain doubts of my substantiality."

"Who have you been with, Jane?"

"You shall not get it out of me to-night, sir; you must wait till to-morrow: to leave my tale half-told, will, you know, be a sort of security that I shall appear at your break-fast-table to finish it. By-the-by, I must mind

not to rise on your hearth with only a glass
of water, then: I must bring an egg at the
least, to say nothing of fried ham."

"You mocking changeling—fairy-born and
human-bred! You make me feel as I have
not felt these twelve months. If Saul could
have had you for his David, the evil spirit
would have been exorcised without the aid of
the harp."

"There, sir, you are redd up and made
decent. Now I'll leave you: I have been
travelling these last three days, and I believe
I am tired. Good-night!"

"Just one word, Jane: were there only
ladies in the house where you have been?"

I laughed and made my escape, still laughing as I ran up stairs. "A good idea!"
I thought, with glee. "I see I have the
means of fretting him out of his melancholy
for some time to come."

Very early the next morning, I heard him
up and astir, wandering from one room to
another. As soon as Mary came down, I
heard the question: "Is Miss Eyre here?"
Then: "Which room did you put her into?
Was it dry? Is she up? Go and ask if she
wants anything; and when she will come
down."

I came down as soon as I thought there was a prospect of breakfast. Entering the room very softly, I had a view of him before he discovered my presence. It was mournful, indeed, to witness the subjugation of that vigorous spirit to a corporeal infirmity. He sat in his chair,—still, but not at rest: expectant evidently ; the lines of now habitual sadness marking his strong features. His countenance reminded one of a lamp quenched, waiting to be relit—and alas ! it was not himself that could now kindle the lustre of animated expression: he was dependent on another for that office ! I had meant to be gay and careless, but the powerlessness of the strong man touched my heart to the quick : still I accosted him with what vivacity I could :—

" It is a bright, sunny morning, sir," I said. " The rain is over and gone, and there is a tender shining after it : you shall have a walk soon."

I had wakened the glow : his features beamed.

" Oh, you are indeed there, my sky-lark ! Come to me. You are not gone: not vanished ? I heard one of your kind an hour ago, singing high over the wood : but its song had no music for me, any more than the rising sun had rays. All the melody on earth is concentrated in my Jane's tongue to my ear: (I am glad it is not naturally a silent one), all the sunshine I can feel is in her presence."

The water stood in my eyes to hear this avowal of his dependence: just as if a royal eagle, chained to a perch, should be forced to entreat a sparrow to become its purveyor But I would not be lachrymose: I dashed off the salt-drops, and busied myself with preparing breakfast.

Most of the morning was spent in the open air. I led him out of the wet and wild wood into some cheerful fields: I described to him how brilliantly green they were; how the flowers and hedges looked refreshed; how sparkingly blue was the sky. I sought a seat for him in a hidden and lovely spot: a dry stump of a tree; nor did I refuse to let him, when seated, place me on his knee: why should I, when both he and I were happier near than apart? Pilot lay beside us: all was quiet. He broke out suddenly while clasping me in his arms:—

"Cruel, cruel deserter! Oh, Jane, what did I feel when I discovered you had fled from Thornfield, and when I could nowhere find you; and, after examining your apartment, ascertained that you had taken no money, nor anything which could serve as an equivalent! A pearl necklace I had given you lay untouched in its little casket; your trunks were left corded and locked as they had been prepared for the bridal tour. What could my darling do, I asked, left destitute and pennyless? And what did she do? Let me hear now."

Thus urged, I began the narrative of my experience for the last year. I softened considerably what related to the three days of wandering and starvation, because to have told him all would have been to inflict unnecessary pain: the little I did say lacerated his faithful heart deeper than I wished.

I should not have left him thus, he said, without any means of making my way: I should have told him my intention. I should have confided in him: he would never have forced me to be his mistress. Violent as he had seemed in his despair, he, in truth, loved me far too well and too tenderly to constitute himself my tyrant: he would have given me half his fortune, without demanding so much as a kiss in return, rather than I should have flung myself friendless on the wide world. I had endured, he was certain, more than I had confessed to him.

"Well, whatever my sufferings had been they were very short," I answered: and then I proceeded to tell him how I had been received at Moor-House; how I had obtained the office of school-mistress, &c. The accession of fortune, the discovery of my relations, followed in due order. Of course, St. John Rivers' name came in frequently in the progress of my tale. When I had done, that name was immediately taken up.

"This St. John, then, is your cousin?"

"Yes."

"You have spoken of him often: did you like him?"

"He was a very good man, sir; I could not help liking him."

"A good man? Does that mean a respectable, well-conducted man of fifty? Or what does it mean?"

"St. John was only twenty-nine, sir."

"*Jeune encore*," as the French say. "Is he a person of low stature, phlegmatic, and plain? A person whose goodness consists rather in his guiltlessness of vice, than in his prowess in virtue?"

" He is untiringly active. Great and exalted deeds are what he lives to perform."

" But his brain? That is probably rather soft? He means well: but you shrug your shoulders to hear him talk?"

" He talks little, sir: what he does say is ever to the point. His brain is first rate, I should think: not impressible, but vigorous."

" Is he an able man, then?"

" Truly able."

" A thoroughly educated man?"

" St. John is an accomplished and profound scholar."

" His manners, I think, you said are not to your taste?—priggish and parsonic?"

" I never mentioned his manners; but, unless I had a very bad taste, they must suit it: they are polished, calm, and gentlemanlike."

" His appearance,—I forget what description you gave of his appearance;—a sort of raw curate, half strangled with his white neck-cloth, and stilted up on his thick-soled high-lows, eh?"

" St. John dresses well. He is a handsome man: tall, fair, with blue eyes, and a Grecian profile."

(*Aside.*) " Damn him!"—(*To me*) " Did you like him, Jane?"

"Yes, Mr. Rochester, I liked him: but you asked me that before."

I perceived, of course, the drift of my interlocutor. Jealousy had got hold of him: she stung him; but the sting was salutary: it gave him respite from the gnawing fang of melancholy. I would not, therefore, immediately charm the snake.

"Perhaps you would rather not sit any longer on my knee, Miss Eyre?" was the next somewhat unexpected observation.

"Why not, Mr. Rochester?"

"The picture you have just drawn is suggestive of a rather too overwhelming contrast. Your words have delineated very prettily a graceful Apollo: he is present to your imagination,—tall, fair, blue-eyed, and with a Grecian profile. Your eyes dwell on a Vulcan,—a real blacksmith, brown, broad-shouldered; and blind and lame into the bargain."

"I never thought of it before; but you certainly are rather like Vulcan, sir."

"Well,—you can leave me, ma'am: but before you go (and he retained me by a firmer grasp than ever), you will be pleased just to answer me a question or two." He paused.

"What questions, Mr. Rochester?"

Then followed this cross-examination : —

"St. John made you school-mistress of Morton before he knew you were his cousin?"

"Yes."

"You would often see him? He would visit the school sometimes?"

"Daily."

"He would approve of your plans, Jane?— I know they would be clever; for you are a talented creature?"

"He approved of them—yes."

"He would discover many things in you he could not have expected to find? Some of your accomplishments are not ordinary."

"I don't know about that."

"You had a little cottage near the school, you say: did he ever come there to see you?"

"Now and then."

"Of an evening?"

"Once or twice."

A pause.

"How long did you reside with him and his sisters after the cousinship was discovered?"

"Five months."

"Did Rivers spend much time with the ladies of his family?"

" Yes; the back parlour was both his study and ours: he sat near the window, and we by the table."

" Did he study much?"

" A good deal."

" What?"

" Hindostanee."

" And what did you do meantime?"

" I learnt German, at first."

" Did he teach you?"

" He did not understand German."

" Did he teach you nothing?"

" A little Hindostanee."

" Rivers taught you Hindostanee?"

" Yes, sir."

" And his sisters also?"

" No."

" Only you?"

" Only me."

" Did you ask to learn?"

" No."

" He wished to teach you?"

" Yes."

A second pause.

" Why did he wish it? Of what use could Hindostanee be to you?"

" He intended me to go with him to India."

" Ah! here I reach the root of the matter. He wanted you to marry him?"

" He asked me to marry him."

" That is a fiction—an impudent invention to vex me."

" I beg your pardon, it is the literal truth: he asked me more than once, and was as stiff about urging his point as ever you could be."

" Miss Eyre, I repeat it, you can leave me. How often am I to say the same thing? Why do you remain pertinaciously perched on my knee, when I have given you notice to quit?".

" Because I am comfortable there."

" No, Jane, you are not comfortable there: because your heart is not with me: it is with this cousin—this St. John. Oh, till this moment, I thought my little Jane was all mine! I had a belief she loved me even when she left me: that was an atom of sweet in much bitter. Long as we have been parted, hot tears as I have wept over our separation, I never thought that while I was mourning her, she was loving another! But it is useless grieving. Jane, leave me: go and marry Rivers."

" Shake me off, then, sir—push me away; for I'll not leave you of my own accord."

" Jane, I ever like your tone of voice: it still renews hope, it sounds so truthful. When

I hear it, it carries me back a year. I forget that you have formed a new tie. But I am not a fool—go——."

" Where must I go, sir?"

" Your own way—with the husband you have chosen."

" Who is that?"

" You know—this St. John Rivers."

"He is not my husband, nor ever will be. He does not love me: I do not love him. He loves (as he *can* love, and that is not as you love) a beautiful young lady called Rosamond. He wanted to marry me only because he thought I should make a suitable missionary's wife, which she would not have done. He is good and great, but severe; and, for me, cold as an iceberg. He is not like you, sir: I am not happy at his side, nor near him, nor with him. He has no indulgence for me—no fondness. He sees nothing attractive in me: not even youth—only a few useful mental points. Then, must I leave you, sir, to go to him?"

I shuddered involuntarily, and clung instinctively closer to my blind but beloved master. He smiled.

" What, Jane! Is this true? Is such really the state of matters between you and Rivers?"

"Absolutely, sir.   Oh, you need not be jealous! I wanted to teaze you a little to make you less sad : I thought anger would be better than grief.   But if you wish me to love you, could you but see how much I *do* love you, you would be proud and content.   All my heart is yours, sir : it belongs to you; and with you it would remain, were fate to exile the rest of me from your presence for ever."

Again, as he kissed me, painful thoughts darkened his aspect.

"My seared vision! My crippled strength!" he murmured regretfully.

I caressed, in order to soothe him.   I knew of what he was thinking, and wanted to speak for him; but dared not.   As he turned aside his face a minute, I saw a tear slide from under the sealed eyelid, and trickle down the manly cheek.   My heart swelled.

"I am no better than the old, lightning-struck chestnut tree in Thornfield orchard;" he remarked, ere long.   "And what right would that ruin have to bid a budding wood-bine cover its decay with freshness?"

"You are no ruin, sir—no lightning-struck tree : you are green and vigorous.   Plants will grow about your roots, whether you ask them or not, because they take delight in your bountiful shadow; and as they grow they will lean towards you, and wind round you, because your strength offers them so safe a prop."

Again he smiled: I gave him comfort.

" You speak of friends, Jane ?" he asked.

" Yes; of friends," I answered rather hesitatingly: for I knew I meant more than friends, but could not tell what other word to employ. He helped me.

" Ah! Jane.   But I want a wife."

" Do you, sir ?"

" Yes: is it news to you ?"

" Of course : you said nothing about it before."

" Is it unwelcome news ?"

" That depends on circumstances, sir—on your choice."

" Which you shall make for me, Jane. will abide by your decision."

" Choose then, sir—*her who loves you best.*"

" I will at least choose—*her I love best.* Jane, will you marry me ?"

" Yes, sir."

" A poor blind man, whom you will have to lead about by the hand ?"

" Yes, sir."

" A crippled man, twenty years older than you, whom you will have to wait on ?"

" Yes, sir."

" Truly, Jane ?"

" Most truly, sir."

" Oh! my darling! God bless you and reward you !"

" Mr. Rochester, if ever I did a good deed in my life—if ever I thought a good thought —if ever I prayed a sincere and blameless prayer—if ever I wished a righteous wish,—I am rewarded now. To be your wife is, for me, to be as happy as I can be on earth."

" Because you delight in sacrifice."

" Sacrifice! What do I sacrifice? Famine for food, expectation for content. To be privileged to put my arms round what I value— to press my lips to what I love—to repose on what I trust: is that to make a sacrifice? If so, then certainly I delight in sacrifice."

" And to bear with my infirmities, Jane: to overlook my deficiencies."

" Which are none, sir, to me. I love you better now, when I can really be useful to you, than I did in your state of proud independence, when you disdained every part but that of the giver and protector."

" Hitherto I have hated to be helped—to be .ed: henceforth, I feel, I shall hate it no more. I did not like to put my hand into a hireling's, but it is pleasant to feel it circled by Jane's little fingers. I preferred utter loneliness to the constant attendance of servants; but Jane's soft ministry will be a perpetual joy. Jane suits me: do I suit her?"

"To the finest fibre of my nature, sir."

"The case being so, we have nothing in the world to wait for: we must be married instantly."

He looked and spoke with eagerness: his old impetuosity was rising.

"We must become one flesh without any delay, Jane: there is but the licence to get—then we marry ——."

"Mr. Rochester, I have just discovered the sun is far declined from its meridian, and Pilot is actually gone home to his dinner. Let me look at your watch."

"Fasten it into your girdle, Janet, and keep it henceforward: I have no use for it."

"It is nearly four o'clock in the afternoon, sir. Don't you feel hungry?"

"The third day from this must be our wedding-day, Jane. Never mind fine clothes and jewels, now: all that is not worth a fillip."

"The sun has dried up all the rain-drops, sir. The breeze is still: it is quite hot."

"Do you know, Jane, I have your little pearl necklace at this moment fastened round my bronze scrag under my cravat? I have worn it since the day I lost my only treasure: as a memento of her."

"We will go home through the wood: that will be the shadiest way."

He pursued his own thoughts without heeding me.

"Jane! you think me, I daresay, an irreligious dog: but my heart swells with gratitude to the beneficent God of this earth just now. He sees not as man sees, but far clearer: judges not as man judges, but far more wisely. I did wrong: I would have sullied my innocent flower—breathed guilt on its purity: the Omnipotent snatched it from me. I, in my stiff-necked rebellion, almost cursed the dispensation: instead of bending to the decree, I defied it. Divine justice pursued its course; disasters came thick on me: I was forced to pass through the valley of the shadow of death. *His* chastisements are mighty; and one smote me which has humbled me for ever. You know I was proud of my strength: but what is it now, when I must give it over to foreign guidance, as a child does its weakness? Of late, Jane—only of late—I began to see

and acknowledge the hand of God in my doom.
I began to experience remorse, repentance; the
wish for reconcilement to my Maker. I began
sometimes to pray: very brief prayers they
were, but very sincere.

"Some days since: nay, I can number
them—four: it was last Monday night, a singular mood came over me: one in which grief
replaced frenzy—sorrow, sullenness. I had
long had the impression that since I could
nowhere find you, you must be dead. Late
that night — perhaps it might be between
eleven and twelve o'clock—ere I retired to
my dreary rest, I supplicated God, that, if it
seemed good to Him, I might soon be taken
from this life, and admitted to that world to
come, where there was still hope of rejoining
Jane.

"I was in my own room, and sitting by the
window, which was open: it soothed me to
feel the balmy night-air; though I could see
no stars, and only by a vague, luminous haze,
knew the presence of a moon. I longed for
thee, Janet! Oh, I longed for thee both with
soul and flesh! I asked of God, at once in
anguish and humility, if I had not been long
enough desolate, afflicted, tormented; and
might not soon taste bliss and peace once

more.   That I merited all I endured, I acknowledged — that I could scarcely endure
more, I pleaded; and the alpha and omega of
my heart's wishes broke involuntarily from my
lips, in the words—" Jane! Jane! Jane!"

"Did you speak these words aloud?"

" I did, Jane.   If any listener had heard
me, he would have thought me mad : I pronounced them with such frantic energy."

"And it was last Monday night : somewhere
near midnight?"

"Yes; but the time is of no consequence :
what followed is the strange point.   You will
think me superstitious — some superstition I
have in my blood, and always had : neverthe-
less, this is true—true at least it is that I heard
what I now relate.

"As I exclaimed 'Jane! Jane! Jane!' a
voice—I cannot tell whence the voice came,
but I know whose voice it was—replied, 'I am
coming : wait for me!' and a moment after,
went whispering on the wind, the words—
'Where are you?'

"I 'll tell you, if I can, the idea, the picture
these words opened to my mind: yet it is
difficult to express what I want to express.
Ferndean is buried, as you see, in a heavy
wood, where sound falls dull, and dies un-

reverberating. 'Where are you?' seemed spoken amongst mountains; for I heard a hill-sent echo repeat the words. Cooler and fresher at the moment the gale seemed to visit my brow: I could have deemed that in some wild, lone scene, I and Jane were meeting. In spirit, I believe, we must have met. You no doubt were, at that hour, in unconscious sleep, Jane: perhaps your soul wandered from its cell to comfort mine; for those were your accents — as certain as I live — they were yours!"

Reader, it was on Monday night — near midnight—that I too had received the mysterious summons: those were the very words by which I had replied to it. I listened to Mr. Rochester's narrative; but made no disclosure in return. The coincidence struck me as too awful and inexplicable to be communicated or discussed. If I told anything, my tale would be such as must necessarily make a profound impression on the mind of my hearer; and that mind, yet from its sufferings too prone to gloom, needed not the deeper shade of the supernatural. I kept these things, then, and pondered them in my heart.

"You cannot now wonder," continued my master, " that when you rose upon me so unexpectedly last night, I had difficulty in believing you any other than a mere voice and vision : something that would melt to silence and annihilation, as the midnight whisper and mountain echo had melted before. Now, I thank God! I know it to be otherwise. Yes, I thank God!"

He put me off his knee, rose, and reverently lifting his hat from his brow, and bending his sightless eyes to the earth, he stood in mute devotion. Only the last words of the worship were audible.

"I thank my Maker, that in the midst of judgment he has remembered mercy. I humbly entreat my Redeemer to give me strength to lead henceforth a purer life than I have done hitherto!"

Then he stretched his hand out to be led. I took that dear hand, held it a moment to my lips, then let it pass round my shoulder: being so much lower of stature than he, I served both for his prop and guide. We entered the wood, and wended homeward.

`

CHAPTER XII.

CONCLUSION.

READER, I married him. A quiet wedding we had: he and I, the parson and clerk, were alone present. When we got back from church, I went into the kitchen of the manor-house, where Mary was cooking the dinner, and John cleaning the knives, and I said:—

"Mary, I have been married to Mr. Rochester this morning." The housekeeper and her husband were both of that decent phlegmatic order of people, to whom one may at any time safely communicate a remarkable piece of news without incurring the danger of having one's ears pierced by some shrill ejaculation, and subsequently stunned by a torrent of wordy wonderment. Mary did look up, and she did stare at me: the ladle with which she was basting a pair of chickens roasting at

the fire, did for some three minutes hang sus-
pended in air ; and for the same space of time
John's knives also had rest from the polishing
process : but Mary, bending again over the
roast, said only :—

" Have you, miss ?   Well, for sure !"

A short time after she pursued : " I seed
you go out with the master, but I didn't know
you were gone to church to be wed ;" and she
basted away.   John, when I turned to him,
was grinning from ear to ear.

" I telled Mary how it would be," he said :
" I knew what Mr. Edward" (John was an old
servant, and had known his master when he
was the cadet of the house, therefore, he often
gave him his christian name)—" I knew what
Mr. Edward would do ; and I was certain he
would not wait long neither : and he's done
right, for aught I know.   I wish you joy,
miss !" and he politely pulled his forelock.

" Thank you, John.   Mr. Rochester told
me to give you and Mary this."   I put into
his hand a five-pound note.   Without waiting
to hear more, I left the kitchen.   In passing
the door of that sanctum some time after, I
caught the words :—

" She'll happen do better for him nor ony
o' t' grand ladies."   And again, " If she be n't

one o' th' handsomest, she's noan faâl and varry good-natured; and i' his een she's fair beautiful, onybody may see that."

I wrote to Moor-House and to Cambridge immediately, to say what I had done: fully explaining also why I had thus acted. Diana and Mary approved the step unreservedly. Diana announced that she would just give me time to get over the honey-moon, and then she would come and see me.

"She had better not wait till then, Jane," said Mr. Rochester, when I read her letter to him; "if she does, she will be too late, for our honey-moon will shine our life-long: its beams will only fade over your grave or mine."

How St. John received the news, I don't know; he never answered the letter in which I communicated it: yet six months after, he wrote to me; without, however, mentioning Mr. Rochester's name, or alluding to my marriage. His letter was then calm; and, though very serious, kind. He has maintained a regular, though not frequent correspondence ever since: he hopes I am happy, and trusts I am not of those who live without God in the world, and only mind earthly things.

You have not quite forgotten little Adèle, have you, reader? I had not; I soon asked and obtained leave of Mr. Rochester, to go and see her at the school where he had placed her. Her frantic joy at beholding me again moved me much. She looked pale and thin : she said she was not happy. I found the rules of the establishment were too strict, its course of study too severe, for a child of her age : I took her home with me. I meant to become her governess once more ; but I soon found this impracticable : my time and cares were now required by another — my husband needed them all. So I sought out a school conducted on a more indulgent system ; and near enough to permit of my visiting her often, and bringing her home sometimes. I took care she should never want for anything that could contribute to her comfort : she soon settled in her new abode, became very happy there, and made fair progress in her studies. As she grew up, a sound, English education corrected in a great measure her French defects ; and when she left school, I found in her a pleasing and obliging companion : docile, good-tempered and well-principled. By her grateful attention to me and mine, she has long since well repaid any little kindness I ever had it in my power to offer her.

My tale draws to its close : one word respecting my experience of married life, and one brief glance at the fortunes of those whose names have most frequently recurred in this narrative, and I have done.

I have now been married ten years. I know what it is to live entirely for and with what I love best on earth. I hold myself supremely blest—blest beyond what language can express; because I am my husband's life as fully as he is mine. No woman was ever nearer to her mate than I am: ever more absolutely bone of his bone, and flesh of his flesh. I know no weariness of my Edward's society: he knows none of mine, any more than we each do of the pulsation of the heart that beats in our separate bosoms; consequently, we are ever together. To be together is for us to be at once as free as in solitude, as gay as in company. We talk, I believe, all day long: to talk to each other is but a more animated and an audible thinking. All my confidence is bestowed on him; all his confidence is devoted to me: we are precisely suited in character; perfect concord is the result.

Mr. Rochester continued blind the first two years of our union: perhaps it was that circumstance that drew us so very near—that knit us so very close; for I was then his vision, as I am still his right hand. Literally, I was (what he often called me) the apple of his eye. He saw nature—he saw books through me; and never did I weary of gazing for his behalf, and of putting into words the effect of field, tree, town, river, cloud, sunbeam—of the landscape before us; of the weather round us—and impressing by sound on his ear what light could no longer stamp on his eye. Never did I weary of reading to him; never did I weary of conducting him where he wished to go: of doing for him what he wished to be done. And there was a pleasure in my services, most full, most exquisite, even though sad—because he claimed these services without painful shame or damping humiliation. He loved me so truly, that he knew no reluctance in profiting by my attendance: he felt I loved him so fondly, that to yield that attendance was to indulge my sweetest wishes.

One morning at the end of the two years, as I was writing a letter to his dictation, he came and bent over me, and said—

"Jane, have you a glittering ornament round your neck?"

I had a gold watch-chain: I answered, "Yes."

"And have you a pale blue dress on?"

I had. He informed me then, that for some

time he had fancied the obscurity clouding one eye was becoming less dense ; and that now he was sure of it.

He and I went up to London. He had the advice of an eminent oculist ; and he eventually recovered the sight of that one eye. He cannot now see very distinctly : he cannot read or write much ; but he can find his way without being led by the hand : the sky is no longer a blank to him—the earth no longer a void. When his first-born was put into his arms, he could see that the boy had inherited his own eyes, as they once were—large, brilliant, and black. On that occasion, he again, with a full heart, acknowledged that God had tempered judgment with mercy.

My Edward and I, then, are happy : and the more so, because those we most love are happy likewise. Diana and Mary Rivers are both married : alternately, once every year, they come to see us, and we go to see them. Diana's husband is a captain in the navy : a gallant officer, and a good man. Mary's is a clergyman : a college friend of her brother's ; and, from his attainments and principles, worthy of the connexion. Both Captain Fitzjames and Mr. Wharton love their wives, and are loved by them.

As to St. John Rivers, he left England : he went to India. He entered on the path he had marked for himself; he pursues it still. A more resolute, indefatigable pioneer never wrought amidst rocks and dangers. Firm, faithful, and devoted ; full of energy, and zeal, and truth, he labours for his race : he clears their painful way to improvement; he hews down like a giant the prejudices of creed and caste that encumber it. He may be stern; he may be exacting; he may be ambitious yet : but his is the sternness of the warrior, Great-heart, who guards his pilgrim-convoy from the onslaught of Apollyon. His is the exaction of the apostle, who speaks but for Christ, when he says—" Whosoever will come after me, let him deny himself, and take up his cross and follow me." His is the ambition of the high master-spirit, which aims to fill a place in the first rank of those who are redeemed from the earth — who stand without fault before the throne of God; who share the last mighty victories of the lamb; who are called, and chosen, and faithful.

St. John is unmarried : he never will marry now. Himself has hitherto sufficed to the toil; and the toil draws near its close : his glorious sun hastens to its setting. The last letter I received from him, drew from my eyes human tears, and yet filled my heart with Divine joy: he anticipated his sure reward, his incorruptible crown. I know that a stranger's hand will write to me next, to say that the good and faithful servant has been called at length into the joy of his Lord. And why weep for this? No fear of death will darken St. John's last hour: his mind will be unclouded; his heart will be undaunted; his hope will be sure; his faith steadfast. His own words are a pledge of this:—

"My Master," he says, "has forewarned me. Daily he announces more distinctly,—'Surely I come quickly;' and hourly I more eagerly respond,—'Amen; even so come, Lord Jesus!'"

FINIS.

29786212R00177

Made in the USA
Middletown, DE
02 March 2016